Ratcatcher

By Viktor Dyk

Translated from the Czech by Roman Kostovski

Plamen
Press

Washington, DC

Plamen Press

1407 Tenth Street NW Washington DC 20001

www.plamenpress.com

Copyright © 2014 Roman Kostovski

Published by Plamen Press 2014

Printed in the United States of America

10 9 8 7 6 5 4 3 2 1

LIBRARY OF CONGRESS CATALOGING-IN-PUBLICATION DATA

Dyk, Viktor.

The Ratcatcher: a novel/Viktor Dyk

p. cm.

ISBN: 978-0-9960722-0-5

Library of Congress Control Number: 2014908076

Translated from the Czech by Roman Kostovski
Cover painting by Anamaria Golemac-Powell
Photography for cover by Jim Marshall

Editors

Rachel Miranda Feingold

Melissa Kostovski

Andrew McIntosh

Jane Meacham

James Morad

The Ratcatcher

Dedicated to Jaroslav Kampr, my friend.

Viktor Dyk

September 1911

I

"And your name is?"

"I have no name. I am nobody. I am less than nobody. I am a ratcatcher."

The man who spoke these words stood with his head held upright in the doorway of a house where the figure of a woman was gleaming in the twilight. He watched her with his dark inquisitive eyes. He was tall and thin and he appeared even thinner in his tight velvet coat and narrow trousers. His hands were small and gentle, like the hands of a lady. He carried no weapon by his side, not even a walking cane, though it seemed as if he came from far away, traveling on roads that weren't always secure. He did, however, hold on to a long, ornamental object that sparked curiosity in the woman with whom he was speaking. It was a unique fife that flaunted the skill of a foreign craftsman. She had never seen anything like it before.

"A ratcatcher," laughed the woman in the doorway. "You've come to Hamelin just in time. There are no ratcatchers here, but we have plenty of rats. Explain to me, Ratcatcher, where do these rats come from? I've been told that they weren't always here. However," she added with a smile, "it's also true that old folks often claim the world keeps getting worse."

The Ratcatcher shrugged.

"I don't know where they come from, but they are in each one of your homes. They continuously gnaw at things, first down in the cellars, in places where you can't see them. But then they grow more daring and climb to the surface. Let's say you plan a feast for a wedding, baptism or something of the sort, and then imagine that during that feast, these rats suddenly appear with their long earlobes and whiskers. You must admit such a view spoils the appetite."

"I agree," the woman laughed. "During Katherine's wedding a big rat suddenly appeared. The groom was pale as a ghost and Katherine fainted. Folks can't bear the sight of anything that would ruin their appetites. That's when they finally decide to call for a ratcatcher."

"Are you preparing a wedding or perhaps a baptism?" the Ratcatcher interrupted suddenly.

The woman in the doorway laughed out loud.

"It's quite obvious that you're a stranger around these parts. No, Ratcatcher, I am not married."

The Ratcatcher bowed.

"It doesn't matter," he said, "it doesn't matter at all... well anyway, people summon the Ratcatcher and he plays and plays his fife until he lures all vermin from their hideouts. They follow him as if they were in a trance, and he leads them to a river: the Rhine, the Danube, the Havel, the Weser... and then the house is free of rats."

The Ratcatcher bowed once more. His voice trembled as if it meant to render an elegy of some sort.

The woman was silent, fidgeting with a twig of jasmine.

"And once the work is done, no one remembers the ratcatcher," he continued. "A ratcatcher, Stranger, is a man who doesn't stay; he leaves. Folks are glad to see him come but are even happier to see him go."

"Is that so?" she said, seemingly encouraging him — or perhaps not. Nevertheless, the Ratcatcher took it as encouragement. His pale cheeks colored, and maybe she would have noticed were it not for the nearing darkness.

"I can sense it, Stranger," he said, "People cannot love a ratcatcher; they can only fear him."

She laughed once again. "What makes the rats follow you so blindly, Ratcatcher?"

He pointed to his fife, which oddly seemed to have come to life. "It's a unique instrument," he said.

She gazed curiously upon the fife and then timidly touched the instrument.

"It's a fife," she said contemptuously, "a pretty fife, but nothing more."

"Rats have good hearing and my fife has a good sound."

The Ratcatcher's eyes ignited with an odd flame. The woman in the doorway stepped back slightly. The twig in her hand began to tremble.

"I have a special talent for purging rats," the Ratcatcher continued, "I sometimes play very sad tunes—songs from all the places I've traveled. And I have seen many places: lands both sunlit and dark, mountains and plains. My fife sounds soft. The rats listen to it and follow. There is no ratcatcher like me anywhere. I will tell you something, beautiful Stranger who laughs like a bell. I have never blown my fife with a full burst of air. I have always softened my blowing. If I gave it all I had, rats would not be the only vermin following me."

The Ratcatcher finished speaking what he wanted to say. The flame in his eyes died out and he intuitively lowered his arms along with his fife.

"I haven't the courage," he added after a moment. "Something cruel would happen."

The young woman stood there silently and never took her eyes off the Ratcatcher or his fife. When he stopped speaking, she said rather quietly,

"I like you, Ratcatcher. Before twilight came, I saw silver streaks in your black hair. Before you spoke, I noticed wrinkles on your forehead. Nevertheless, I like what I see. Surely, many women have loved you."

"Perhaps," the Ratcatcher replied. "I don't remember." His words developed a strange, resonant accent that captivated the woman. Her tone grew serious. She leaned toward him so she could feel his hot breath.

"I like you, Ratcatcher," she continued encouragingly. "But if I were you, I would blow into that fife with all the breath I had."

"Do you realize what could happen?" the Ratcatcher asked in a gloomy voice. "I don't know myself. All I can tell you is that, time after time, anguish consumes me. I look at my fife as upon something that has destroyed many and is meant to destroy even more. And then I laugh. It is nothing more than a pretty fife. You said it yourself. I am nothing more than a ratcatcher who is destined to lead away all unwanted guests. A ratcatcher is like Ahasver,[1] who travels from town to town, from North to South, from East to West; and just like Ahasver, he can't stand still. Have I outstayed my welcome here, Stranger? Should I go?"

---

1 *Translator's note*: Ahasver is better known in medieval Central European mythology as the *Wandering Jew*.

"No," she said. And then she began to whisper. "You can call me Agnes."

"Agnes," he said, and as he spoke his voice turned soft and melodic. His lips gathered a peculiar sense of magic.

She looked at him intensely.

"Will you be leaving Hamelin soon?"

"I don't know," he said. "It is not up to me. And..."

He then replied with a glance.

She laughed and it sounded fresh and pure — filled with youth and happiness. It resonated like the bells of resurrection.

"I think that you have your work cut out for you. There are many rats here." Then she added in a more serious tone, "You should stay, Ratcatcher."

He did not answer. Their eyes met. She felt uneasy yet gazed inquisitively into his fiery eyes. The jasmine twig trembled in her hand.

"I have a lover," she said.

The Ratcatcher took her by the hand.

"I don't want to see him. I don't want to hear anything about him. I know that there are many ugly things in this world. Why do I need to care about them if they don't cross my path? However, if I did meet him..."

The Ratcatcher's voice grew deep and then

saddened. It sounded serious and threatening like a passing bell.

"No," she sighed, but it wasn't clear to him what that word meant. They both found themselves at the edge of a steep crevice where neither dared to take that extra step; where flight was the only alternative. He held her hand in his own and she allowed him to. He squeezed it. He squeezed her with a force and passion that made her gasp in pain. Nevertheless, she returned the gesture and the pain he felt was numbing.

"Agnes," he said and it sounded like a question as well as a plea. She looked at him and smiled.

"Yes," she replied, and it was clear to him what that word meant. It was utterly naked, without timidity or reservation. And the woman in the doorway handed the Ratcatcher her twig of jasmine.

Viktor Dyk

II

When the Ratcatcher awoke, he found himself in a small refuge in the good Hanseatic[2] town of Hamelin, a quiet and abandoned sanctuary separated from the town's presence. Heavy wagons loaded with merchandise never rumbled here. No one would hear the bustle of markets or the sound of riders dressed in lavish armor traveling through. Not even religious processions would pass by. Only the ringing of bells from the Holy Trinity Cathedral in Hamelin made its way to this place. Their voice was deep and pensive, but it was rather forgettable to those who heard it so often. At least Agnes, when she opened her window, would hear different voices.

There was a garden in bloom beneath her window, where birds would sing to her and everything buzzed with life and laughter as she greeted each day. The garden carried so many fragrances — each was

---

2 *Translator's note*: *Hanseatic* means part of the Hanseatic League, a commercial and defensive confederation of merchant guilds and their market towns that dominated trade throughout Northern Europe. The town of Hamelin was a member of this league.

intoxicating. And Agnes thought she was a flower among flowers and a fragrance among fragrances.

Agnes lived in a house with a hollow tile roof. It was an old house covered in the green of chestnut trees, but it had the ability to brighten when unveiled in the sunlight.

Then there was beautiful Agnes's mother—a woman wilted more by the sadness of her stories than by the years that had passed. They were stories that she remembered with a blend of nostalgia and horror. She would tremble feverishly as she hovered like a ghost around the house. The sun and the light would scare her and she would run from them like a nocturnal bird.

Agnes, on the other hand, did not seem to be afraid of anything. She would gaze upon the future armed with a credulous smile.

And so the days went by, and the Ratcatcher stayed in Hamelin chasing rats away.

It was quite the event for Hamelin. Children and old folks alike would accompany him on his route. Children and old folks alike would become baffled by the way the rats would blindly follow the Ratcatcher to their demise. They were fascinated by his fife, which to these good and honorable citizens sounded no louder than a distant buzzing of insects.

The river waves embraced the rats and consumed

them. Then they carried them to the sea — the faraway sea — never again to spoil the fine appetites of the respectable citizens of this Hanseatic town.

The Ratcatcher continued to lure the rats away, but he also had another reason to extend his stay in Hamelin...

III

Down where the Wesser and Havel rivers merged there lived a fisherman by the name of Sepp Jörgen. He had a small and destitute house and he lived a poor and wretched life.

People of all the guilds in Hamelin would ridicule the poor lad, for he had difficulty understanding things. He was kind, but rather dense. They said that he would laugh or cry, but it would always occur a day later, and they were right.

When it came to fishing, he didn't have to think. He'd toss his nets and then wait. Waiting was the one thing Sepp Jörgen could do like no other. He would wait patiently, resigned to his fate, but he would rarely see anything happen as a result. They say that those who wait like this are destined to such an existence.

Sepp Jörgen, however, never lost his patience. He knew that day must look like day and night must look like night; that some folks were born into happiness and others into despair. He knew that there were noblemen at the Town Hall dressed in lavish furs and beautiful chains who gave orders. There were also the poor living in dark and damp lairs who had to follow these orders. He understood this because he saw it his entire life.

He knew that he had to avoid the imperial road when he saw drunken *landsknechts* coming.[3] He knew these things though he was a slow lad.

Eventually, he realized that everyone was laughing at him. His fellow fishermen, the girls in Hamelin. It would hurt him, and in due time it seemed hard for Jörgen to determine what hurt him more. His fists were often clenched, but his heart was, too. Unfortunately, because of his shortcomings, Sepp Jörgen would always realize these feelings a day later. And so men would calmly walk away after insulting him and women who had the potential to love him would fade into the distance. It was his destiny, and no one escapes destiny.

And yet, Sepp Jörgen was a stout lad with strong muscles and firm fists. He was handsome with a good heart and kind but rather unruly eyes.

The only thing he owned was a thrush in a cage, which he cared for meticulously. He knew how to do this because the task was simple and plain. Day

---

3 *Translator's note: Landsknechts* were mercenary soldiers active in fifteenth- and sixteenth-century Europe. They were mostly foot soldiers and pike-men.

after day it was the same, and day after day it was beautiful — at least it seemed that way to Jörgen. The thrush did not laugh at him or hurt him, and if the Fisherman felt sad and lonely, the thrush was capable of easing his rather foolish heart. Jörgen would listen to its clear and soothing song. He would forget about his terrible catch, his poverty and the insults of all the beautiful girls living in Hamelin. He would smile, lulled by song, and everything would smile upon his wretched life. In this world women would come and kiss him.

The bird would sing and Sepp Jörgen would live expecting nothing more out of life.

IV

The lover's name was Kristian. They called him Tall
Kristian. He had blond hair, blue eyes and everything
a citizen of Hamelin could wish for—honorable
parents, a good name, respect for both the Town Hall
and the Church. He was employed in his uncle's store
located in the archway of Hamelin's town square.
It was a draper's shop that was well-known far and
near, and because Kristian's uncle was childless, his
nephew cherished the thought that he would become
the sole heir of this enterprise. The only rub was that
Uncle Andreas, a somewhat older man, never stopped
pursuing affairs that only a merchant such as him
could afford—affairs that scandalized the respectable
name of the town. Tall Kristian did what he could to
lure all temptation from his uncle's path. He acquired
the services of Miss Gertrude, a woman older and no
longer attractive, to be his uncle's housekeeper. Uncle
Andreas had little time to pursue his lovers, so Kristian
teetered between hope and despair. Besides that, he
loved Agnes.

He would tell her about his worries and sleepless nights when the thought of a temptress troubled him like a nightmare. He would tell her about his uncle's affairs with a disgust that only a respectable man and threatened heir could render.

Agnes would listen. Her only worry was to keep the Ratcatcher a secret from Kristian and to make sure that one would never be seen by the other.

Kristian would sometimes talk about the Ratcatcher, his accomplishments, and his trade, which the draper's nephew considered to be useful but not highly regarded. Agnes would listen and agree — at least that was how Kristian interpreted her silence.

The Ratcatcher remained in Hamelin and Tall Kristian continued to teeter between hope and despair.

V

Above the beautiful Hanseatic town of Hamelin stood Koppel Mountain, a source of pride that was equal only to the pride the townspeople had for Hamelin itself. On Sundays the townspeople would dress festively, leave the gates of Hamelin and set off to ascend Koppel Mountain. The climb was steep and sweat dripped down their foreheads, but the view from the top of the city and its surroundings was well worth the effort.

During the climb, they had to pass through a dark pine forest and though the citizens of Hamelin never realized it, the forest was rather sad. But even the saddest forest could not retain its woe when it was filled with the joyous and thoughtful conversations of Hamelin's merchants and their respectable wives, as well as the local girls and boys.

Above this wooded area, which to most citizens represented the final stage of their climb, Koppel Mountain offered other possibilities. If you suddenly left the forest, you would pass by several scattered boulders that made their way to this place centuries ago. Everything there was large and plain. You would then have a seat and take in the view of the town, warm yourself in the sun and enjoy the Sunday tranquility because if you journeyed farther, you'd come to the edge of a giant abyss. The open abyss was cold and deep, and its bottom seemed endless. If you threw a stone, it would fall for a very long time. Koppel's top had its secrets. It was not simply an abyss but also a road — at least several brave souls claimed this after venturing all the way to Koppel's crest to explore the mysteries of its peak.

No one knew for certain, but folks would say this road led deep beneath the earth, far beyond the mountains and rivers to the land of the Seven Castles. They would claim this in spite of the fact that they never remembered who told them this story in the first place. One thing was certain: No one had ever completed this courageous journey and no one had ever reached the land of the Seven Castles from the top of Koppel Mountain.

One day the Ratcatcher stood above this abyss. He journeyed through the pine forest and the bare mountaintop where local snakes were sunning themselves. The Ratcatcher felt a craving to continue this journey. He stood at the edge, venturing farther than any of those brave souls born in Hamelin ever dared. He stood at that edge and it seemed as if he was speaking to the abyss — that mistress to all *felones-de-se*.[4]

It was clear that the abyss was tempting the Ratcatcher to go beyond its edge. He stood above it, alone and pensive. The townspeople of Hamelin would not have appreciated the look he had in his eyes — a look that was deep and bottomless, and at that moment there was not just one abyss at the peak of Koppel Mountain, but rather two.

---

4 *Translator's note*: *felones-de-se* are those who commit suicide.

VI

One day Sepp Jörgen lay in a meadow near his cottage. His head leaned on a pile of hay that smelled good, and Jörgen soon fell into a deep and unconscious sleep. Meanwhile two girls from Hamelin happened to stray onto Jörgen's meadow. It was Lora, Woodcarver Wolfram's daughter, and Kätchen, the daughter of Grill, the baker. They both had blond hair and curious eyes and they were intoxicated by youth. They were laughing because they were beautiful and they were beautiful because they were laughing. The sleeping fisherman ignited a curiosity within them. Tiptoeing, they closed in and began to study his face. The sleeping lad did not hear their footsteps. His torso was rising and dropping in a steady rhythm. His shirt was partially undone, and the girls could see his hairy and rather large, angular chest.

Lora Wolfram sat down next to the sleeping man. She leaned over him with her supple body as she held her breath to avoid waking him. But such measures were unnecessary. Sepp Jörgen never woke up. Kätchen also mustered the confidence to lightly touch the lad's curly hair with her soft hand. He quivered slightly, as if he were touched by something cold and ugly, but Kätchen's hands were neither cold nor ugly. On the contrary, she was known by everyone in Hamelin for her beautiful hands.

But Sepp Jörgen did not awaken in spite of this quivering. The girls' eyes ignited with a peculiar flame. This man lying there indifferently and in such close proximity sparked an interest while he was sleeping — an interest that would have never occurred if he were awake. It seemed that everything trivial, ridiculous and petty linked to this lad's name, was slipping away. All that remained was the man resting on a pile of hay.

"If only it weren't Jörgen," Kätchen noted and shrugged her shoulders.

The woodcarver's daughter Lora Wolfram repeated, "If only it weren't Jörgen."

They lingered over the sleeping fisherman for a while as desire — and perhaps even gentleness — incited uncertain dreams of lust and love. A wave of intoxication overpowered their young bodies. Something was forcing them into the arms of the strong and muscular man.

The hay with a blend of scythed wild flowers smelled good.

"If only it weren't Jörgen," Kätchen repeated with a touch of regret, "it would be possible to love him. He is not ugly and surely only a few could match his strength. Folks say that no one should mess with Jörgen."

"A day later," Lora added. "He does everything a day later. If he ever gets married, he is bound to realize the next day that he has a wife. The poor thing will have a terrible wedding night."

Lora's words, followed by suppressed laughter, finally woke the sleeping fisherman. At first, he looked around uneasily. He was comprehending neither time nor space. He stared at the girls' flustered faces with a strange and baffled look in his eyes. The Hamelin girls could no longer hold back their unruly nature. They burst into excessive laughter that was heard from far away — a laughter that was healthy, tangible, and overindulgent. It was the laughter of a woman who would like to sin.

The Fisherman stared baffled and mute at the laughing girls. Then slowly he began to get up, gazing at Kätchen and Lora. But enough was enough. The girls realized that it would be unwise to be caught in the presence of Sepp Jörgen, especially because his foolishness began to resurface. They disappeared before Jörgen could come to fully. Nevertheless, one could hear their untamed laughter from far away. Sepp Jörgen still did not understand what was happening. It was his destiny not to understand.

VII

The night was damp and moonlit. The square in Hamelin was empty. A watchman passed by a noticeable old fountain with statues of Neptune and Triton, another source of pride for the townspeople of Hamelin. The watchman disappeared somewhere in the archway, and the evening grew quiet.

It was only by Woodcarver Wolfram's doorway — and honorable Master Baker Grill had his shop there as well — that something resembling a man was cowering in the dark. It looked somewhat devastated and inhuman. It had eyes, such eager eyes, focused only in one particular direction.

When the watchman sounded the midnight hour in the distance, Andreas, the draper, passed through the archway heading for a tryst with one of the women at the Holy Spirit Tavern. His footsteps disturbed the silence of the night, but the devastated creature paid no attention to him.

Then the watchman passed by again and a sudden interest hastened his steps. But before he approached this distraught being, the watchman's expectation and awareness ebbed. He shrugged his shoulders and went about his business. There was no prospect of an earning here. None. For it was only Sepp Jörgen.

Sepp did not speak. He gazed upon the woodcarver's door as if he could open it with his sight. The door, however, was well locked. The woodcarver, Wolfram, and baker, Grill, were most likely asleep. Perhaps Kätchen and Lora were as well. Their windows were closed and they had no plans to open them. A juvenile attempt to wake the two girls would never have crossed Sepp Jörgen's mind anyway. Surely, there were enough tiny pebbles well-suited to draw attention, but it was pointless to wake a woman who had no wish to be roused. Even the dim Sepp Jörgen understood this.

Sepp Jörgen was not moving, but this did not mean that he was there waiting idly. Suddenly, the Ratcatcher's tall and misshapen shadow appeared from behind the Fisherman.

The Ratcatcher was wandering the streets. He was having one of his restless nights. He leaned over Sepp Jörgen, who was mumbling quiet yet passionate words:

"Go ahead and laugh. Yes, laugh at Sepp Jörgen. I know you! You're Lora, Woodcarver Wolfram's daughter. You are Kätchen, the daughter of Baker

Grill. You're both beautiful and you're more beautiful when you laugh. It's useless to tell you this because you know it very well. Yet, there is one thing you don't know and Sepp Jörgen will tell you. You laugh, but it is not wise to laugh at a man, even if he is only Sepp Jörgen. It's true that I am slow, that I am telling you now what I should have told you yesterday. You disappeared before I could express my pain. You don't listen to me when I speak. I missed my opportunity as I always do. Many people have laughed at me because of this, but no laughter is more crushing than that of a woman. Oh, the way you laughed at me! The blood in my veins boiled and my fists were clenched hard! I might be just a fisherman, but I have hands that could easily strangle a beautiful neck—a pale and beautiful neck—like yours I imagine.

"Why did you come to my meadow? I didn't call for you and I wasn't even looking or waiting for you.

"You came and you leaned over my face. I was dreaming. I had beautiful rosy dreams—the kind I get when my thrush is singing. But I have to tell you that I have no thrush now. I strangled the creature. It was the only thing I've ever owned and it will never sing again. It will never comfort me. My cottage will be silent and lifeless. I tested the strength of my hands. It was so satisfying to strangle something.

"I awoke from my dream. Oh, what a sharp laughter you have! As if a thousand devils were laughing, and not just two women! It is not wise to laugh at a man, even if he is only Jörgen. Now it's nighttime and you are asleep, but what if morning comes and Jörgen never leaves this place? Who is to say that this cursed laughter will stop haunting my ears? If it doesn't, woe to you, Lora and Kätchen! My thrush is dead. Everything that I have ever owned is dead. All I hear is laughter — sharp hellish laughter!"

The Ratcatcher gently touched the Fisherman's shoulder.

"Stand up, Jörgen."

The Fisherman gazed at him with a dull and confused look in his eyes. What on earth did this ratcatcher want with him?

"Stand up, Jörgen," the Ratcatcher continued. "I have traveled many lands and visited many towns. That is why I tell you to stand up. It is not good to be on your knees."

The Fisherman continued to gaze at him with a dull and confused look. The expression on his face did not change.

"Your Kätchen and your Lora will not hear you. They are sleeping. If they did hear you, your chances would be worse, Sepp Jörgen. A man who is on his knees is not a man."

But Sepp Jörgen did not listen. He gazed somewhere — into a window, or perhaps into emptiness.

"If you'd like, Jörgen, I will tell you the honest truth. There is only a certain measure of love between two people. It is limited and invariable. Never love excessively if you want to be loved back. If you do, you alone will exhaust all the affection meant for two. An overload of what you give kills the hope for what you should receive. This is advice from the Ratcatcher, who has seen many things. Be the man you want, just don't allow a woman to have you when it is *you* who should have her. Be who you want, but don't be cruel about it. That is unnecessarily harsh, Fisherman. But if you are kind by nature, try to hide it. Stand up, Jörgen."

But Jörgen did not move.

The tower on the Holy Trinity Cathedral struck the hour.

The Ratcatcher shook his head indifferently. He pitied the devastated face kneeling at the deaf door of Woodcarver Wolfram, but he could not help.

"Farewell, Jörgen. You are a lost cause," he said after a little while. "You will never be happy. Does it matter after all? Happiness is not the pinnacle of life. Perhaps you are destined for something better if it doesn't involve happiness."

And the Ratcatcher began to leave.

It didn't seem that the Fisherman noticed his departure. Sepp Jörgen understood things too late. He kept mumbling something sad and monotonous into the silence of the night. He babbled words of love and hate, promises and threats. But they echoed through the darkness to no avail.

The Ratcatcher, in the meantime, headed for a quiet little street, to the house where Agnes lived. He tapped on her window. The window opened and soon after it was followed by the door.

VIII

On Sundays after Mass, the Thirsty Man Tavern was lively and full of noise. It was the most popular and frequented establishment that the Hanseatic town of Hamelin had to offer. Nowhere far or near could a patron drink better wine, and the tavern's cook, Black Liza, had culinary skills that could compete with the best. Not even the county's aldermen could deny themselves a visit to the tavern's arched dining room. There was a table reserved for them at all times and it was well-guarded against imposters. Noble citizens were always the first to taste newly arrived barrels. They were also the ones who provided important and decisive input on matters of both cuisine and public opinion.

The Thirsty Man Tavern was a place where business deals were commonly brokered because it was only there that the cautious and prudent citizens of Hamelin would warm to one another. Wedding engagements were settled at the tavern because only there could the cautious and prudent citizens of Hamelin begin to contemplate matters of love, even if this love was about as true as an eagle is true to a sparrow. If a citizen of Hamelin was struck by sorrow, he would go and have a drink at Konrad Röger's place. That was the name of the tavern's portly innkeeper, a kind man who never refused to indulge in the spoils of his own cellar. If there was a joyous occasion, that also gave reason to drink at Konrad Röger's, for no one else could spread joy so rampantly. Baptisms were celebrated at the tavern as if Röger was hosting the event in his own house. Name days were celebrated there, and they seemed as if Röger himself was celebrating his own. If a patron needed to drink in peace, no one could arrange it better than Röger. If someone needed to hear a story, the innkeeper knew the most capricious and frolicsome tales a man could tell.

An innkeeper is somewhat of a confessor. He respects the vow of silence, but there are never any unveiled secrets or mysteries he doesn't know. Röger knew how to look upon his fellow citizens with joyful and compassionate eyes. He was a humble man who could have accomplished many things, if he had had the ambition. However, Konrad Röger wanted nothing more than the pleasure of owning the Thirsty Man Tavern. There were rumors of an affair with Black Liza, but when could an innkeeper find the time to sin? His days and nights, his laughter and his tears—all were devoted to the patrons of his tavern.

There were taverns where patrons would quarrel and brawls soon broke out. However, Konrad Röger's guests quarreled very rarely and not once did they ever have a physical altercation. The tavern's dining room offered a soothing and peaceful atmosphere. People would enter this establishment inflamed in disputes, yet somehow the tavern would change their attitudes. Soon, there would be no sign of a quarrel. And it wasn't because the disputing parties settled their differences or because they made peace with each other. The next morning or perhaps even that same night, when they left the tavern, stepping out into the fresh air, they would realize that neither of them was any closer to an agreement. But in the meantime the tavern offered a sanctuary where everything seemed rosy.

There were folks in Hamelin who were (or perhaps weren't) ashamed to admit that they had never climbed Koppel Mountain, but there wasn't a soul in town who had never been to the Thirsty Man Tavern. There were folks in Hamelin who were (or perhaps weren't) ashamed to admit that they didn't know the name of their alderman or even the town's leader, Bürgermeister Dörrick. However, everyone knew Konrad Röger.

That Sunday, two honorable and prudent neighbors were sitting at the table reserved for the town's aldermen. The first one, Gottlieb Frosch, was a carpenter renowned for his ability to serve anyone in Hamelin and beyond. He had six apprentices in his workshop and Gottlieb Frosch, though an alderman, could also put his own hands to work, if circumstances required it. Frosch's name meant quality work. He was a huge man, almost the size of a giant, and various stories about his strength would circulate around Hamelin from time to time.

Frosch's neighbor, Boniface Strumm, was smaller and thinner, and he was a tailor by trade. Strumm was also known throughout the area. Rumor had it that wealthy merchants would come from as far as Hannover and put their faith into the skilled hands and trained eye of Boniface Strumm. There was talk that the tailor employed journeymen who sailed across the sea and traveled from as far as the Rhine and the Danube to work with him. That was how strongly people gravitated toward Boniface Strumm, whose artistic skill and mastery became an unattainable objective for hundreds of hopeful dreamers who sought to fulfill their ambitions by emulating this famous tailor.

It was therefore obvious that Röger would devote all his attention to these two respectable citizens. He tried to read the most hidden of wishes in their eyes. He was meticulously mindful of any haze of displeasure that could cloud the tavern's atmosphere, and he saw to it that it evaporated as soon as possible. Röger could be many people at once and yet, when it was necessary, he knew how to be invisible. Meanwhile, the Ratcatcher was sitting at a table not too far from the aldermen's. He sat alone.

The citizens of Hamelin weren't sure how to relate to the Ratcatcher. It was clear that he provided a valuable service. They knew that his fife had remarkable powers. Yet, there was something inexplicable that raised their suspicion. For instance, they knew nothing about him. They wondered whether his friendship was honorable and his path was righteous. They could not comprehend a power that ruled over something as ugly and insolent as a rat. It was unclear whether a priest had blessed his fife, and even if one had, what sort of priest was he? There was too much uncertainty at stake and the citizens of Hamelin loved things that were certain. That was why the Ratcatcher sat alone at his table. He could have observed all of this; however, he paid no attention to his surroundings. He was drinking quietly but he hadn't come to this tavern without a purpose.

His purpose was simple. At the beginning of his

stay in Hamelin, the Ratcatcher visited the Town Hall. He presented his fife and offered to lure all the rats away from town. At that time the vermin were so daring they didn't even spare the Town Hall. One rat bearing an ugly resemblance to the rodent that paid homage to maid Katherine's wedding interrupted the dignity of a prominent and important aldermen's meeting in Hamelin. That was the final straw, and the town decided to seek revenge against the rats and call for a ratcatcher. The townspeople, who perhaps in the heat of passion didn't factor in all the details, agreed to compensate the Ratcatcher with a sum of money that later seemed excessive after the rats had gone. It was one hundred Rhine ducats, a disproportionate sum considering the small measure of effort required for the Ratcatcher to complete his task.

That day the Ratcatcher was determined to remind the aldermen of their obligations. Because he knew it was customary to discuss business at the Thirsty Man, approaching the aldermen in the tavern did not seem inappropriate to him. However, one should also understand that this was a communal matter, worthy of special protocol, and if it was appropriate to remind Peter to pay Paul, it certainly wasn't fitting to remind an alderman to pay up in such a public place.

But the Ratcatcher, perhaps encouraged by wine,

did not take such etiquette into consideration. He stood up and headed straight for the aldermens' table.

"I am the Ratcatcher," he said and he bowed in front of Frosch and Strumm.

Both aldermen were somewhat startled by the Ratcatcher's rudeness, but it was unbecoming of a town leader to express such a reaction in public. And so they settled for something that resembled a slight nod but no one could actually tell whether it was a nod at all. The citizens of Hamelin loved things that were clear.

"I am the Ratcatcher," the man continued rudely. "I have fulfilled my obligation. It has been a while since the last of the rats have floated into the sea, but I have not yet received my Rhine ducats."

The Thirsty Man was suddenly overwhelmed with silent tension. The situation was completely unexpected. No one had ever dared to speak to Frosch and Strumm in this manner. Everyone held his or her breath and anxiously waited for the next moment.

But Frosch and Strumm were not easily ruffled. They were even willing to overlook such inappropriate comments. Frosch simply shrugged his shoulders, and nimble Strumm began in a serious and dignified manner to reiterate the reasoning that was given to them a day earlier in Hamelin's town council by a learned and wise man who was well-versed in law and traditions.

"This contract of which you speak is, above all, incomplete and therefore not valid, even though one of the parties in agreement, namely the town of Hamelin, has been acknowledged by law. On the other hand, the party who is to receive payment," Strumm the tailor hesitated for an instant, but after a gulp of wine continued, "has been neither accurately nor legally verified. One could even say that this person is completely unknown to the people of Hamelin and its surroundings. Because it has been never determined that you are the individual who forged this contract with the town of Hamelin, there is no other option than to postpone compensation until your identity is confirmed. In the event that your identity is verified, by law the contract still could not be considered complete because, according to local customs and traditions, the necessary phrase 'May God help us' was not uttered upon conclusion of the agreement. And many witnesses can testify to Hamelin authorities that this particular phrase is customary and essential to the validity of any settlement."

Tailor Strumm took another gulp and then let out a deep breath. It didn't seem that he was very confident at holding his ground, so Gottlieb Frosch determined that it was a good time to mediate.

"Nevertheless," Frosch said deliberately. "In the likelihood that your identity can be verified, I am of the opinion that you should receive a salary. If you were to sensibly lower your demands, I am willing to present your reasonable claim to the council and support it. Surely you can acknowledge that it is not so complicated to chase away rats, and you shouldn't have overestimated such a task. You play your fife and the rats follow. When I build a bed on which you can sleep, it takes a great deal of toil and work. Nevertheless, my workshop is my life. I create beds, cradles and even coffins. It is the whole world to me, Ratcatcher."

Boniface Strumm, however, did not want to give Frosch the final word.

"The clothes make the man," he said finally. "Without them, man looks and acts like an animal. If there were no clothes, how could we recognize a priest from an alderman? If women wore nothing, how could we distinguish a respectable one from a harlot? Once a man puts on clothes, he truly becomes a man. Once someone like *yourself* dresses in clothing made by Boniface Strumm, he will *almost* look like a citizen of this honorable merchant town of Hamelin. Could there be anything better than that, Ratcatcher?"

The patrons of the Thirsty Man were surprised by the restraint of the two aldermen, whose gentle and deliberate words dismissed the Ratcatcher's inappropriate request. But the Ratcatcher did not appreciate such compassion. His cheeks turned red; he stood up and waved his right hand.

"I *am* the Ratcatcher!" he shouted abruptly, and those present at the tavern realized that the outside windows were trembling. "I am the Ratcatcher and you recognize who I am! There is no one like me, and I don't know if there ever will be. I fulfilled my end of the bargain. You did not! I warn you, tread lightly!"

The patrons were surprised once again at the restraint shown by the two aldermen. Not even the Ratcatcher's last statement upset them. Gottlieb Frosch then spoke in such a quiet and soothing voice that the patrons could not hear his words.

"I do not doubt that you will succeed in proving your identity. I offered you my help. If you would accept your salary in the form of products from my workshop—you would find everything there needed for life and death—we could perhaps reach an agreement."

"It would also be highly possible," Boniface Strumm added, "that your claim would be considered if you accepted half of your salary in products from my workshop. Boniface Strumm is known throughout all of Germany. It is only up to you to help yourself to what you are entitled."

But after these rather quiet words—barely comprehensible to those who were listening—the Ratcatcher exploded only more outrageously. He disregarded any respectful courtesy traditionally bestowed upon an alderman and he slammed his fist on their table so hard that a glass fell and spilled its remaining wine.

"You say that the words *'May God help us'* were missing. There is no need for God's help! I will help myself."

And with these blasphemous words the Ratcatcher left the tavern.

Viktor Dyk

IX

The Ratcatcher was nervously pacing across the room and Agnes watched him with her wide pupils. She could not take her eyes off his steps. He was handsome in his anger. His eyes were burning with an unsettled flame and all his movements became beautiful. To Agnes, he seemed as if he were growing larger. She instinctively curled up deeper into the corner by her window. Surprisingly, there was nothing frightening about her fear. It was rather intoxicating. Grow larger, Ratcatcher! Beautiful Agnes awaits you!

The Ratcatcher was still nervously pacing the room. Its low ceiling could not contain this angry man. The whole world would not be enough. He did not complain and he did not threaten, but his silence was even more terrifying. Boniface Strumm and Gottlieb Frosch, though respected aldermen of this town, would have never repeated their earlier offers to this silent man. The Ratcatcher did not gesticulate, and his steps were neither heavy nor loud. So what caused this silent pacing to be so disturbing?

Agnes was curled up for a long time. She dared not move or utter a word. She was afraid of the Ratcatcher's unknown power. She could not understand it but she would yield to it instantly. Agnes was afraid of him but she loved her fear. She loved the Ratcatcher as well.

Did she love Tall Kristian? Perhaps she loved him yesterday. Perhaps she will love him tomorrow. However, at that moment he was not in this room. He wasn't even in her heart.

No one could love like Agnes and no one could forget like her. After a night of lovemaking, she would wake up with eyes innocent as a child's. If anyone asked her, she would simply and convincingly respond, "Nothing happened."

Agnes feared this particular moment and adored it at the same time. Her fear was also her passion.

Suddenly, in an unexpected gesture — one that bore the comfort of a mother and the flattery of a lover — she embraced the Ratcatcher's neck. The Ratcatcher trembled as he was touched by her naked hands, and that tremor encouraged his hesitant soul.

"Ratcatcher," Agnes implored soothingly.

The silence was disturbed and the enchantment disappeared. The courageous Ratcatcher returned from his angry flight and landed on the humble soil of Hamelin. He was smiling upon his return. All that had absorbed him a moment ago, all that tortured his thoughts, seemed trivial and empty. He embraced Agnes with arms of steel and he spoke, gazing into her promising eyes with passion and humility.

"I could annihilate Hamelin! Destroy Frosch and Strumm! I could ensure that not a single soul would remain inside these city walls. I am capable of this. Yet I don't want to do it. God requested seven fair-minded men to save Sodom and Gomorra! I wish to be more modest than God. All I need is a single fair-minded woman. I will spare Hamelin for your sake, Agnes!"

His face touched hers. His body caressed hers. Agnes felt an intoxicating joy. The Ratcatcher belonged to her. She realized the validity of her power. Her eyes twinkled with a confidence that flowed into her heart like the scent of a May evening flows into the opening of a bedroom window.

Agnes's heart calmed, though it had been pounding vigorously a few moments ago. It was no longer filled with fear.

A few moments earlier Agnes was under the impression the Ratcatcher was growing in a sullen and anxious manner. Now it was she who was growing.

X

That night in Hamelin was truly bizarre. Gottlieb Frosch was ambushed by strange nightmares. He dreamed that he was laboring away in his famous workshop. He had been commissioned to make one thousand beds of quality wood. It was an order directly from the royal palace. Oh how noisy and joyful it was! Gottlieb Frosch was working and overseeing the project. He was determined to finish that day, no matter what the cost. Not a single second could go to waste. The journeymen would receive a special bonus if they completed the job on time.

And behold, the job was finished according to plan! Gottlieb Frosch knew his people. The work was done. The alderman looked around his workshop proudly. He began to count until he could count no more. He then let out a confident laugh. Suddenly, he realized that he was not the only one laughing. The Ratcatcher was standing across from him. Frosch felt somewhat unpleasant and he tried to overcome the feeling.

"Here is your special bonus," he said to Wolfgang,

his head journeyman. "You've all earned it."

And the master carpenter padded the journeyman on his back. But the Ratcatcher refused to walk away. He was laughing and it seemed to Frosch that the devil himself was laughing.

The devil was a weakness of Gottlieb Frosch's. He never liked to speak of the devil, perhaps because he thought of him so often. He tried to overcome this weakness. He stared the Ratcatcher proudly in the face. Had he not just defended the good reputation of his factory? He managed to express all the pride of that moment in three words:

"One thousand beds," he said.

The Ratcatcher did not take his eyes off the alderman. He never stopped laughing. Frosch's pride was melting away beneath this burning laughter. But Frosch was not used to backing down so easily.

"A thousand beds," he repeated, "commissioned by the king. Only Frosch could handle such a project."

"A thousand coffins," the Ratcatcher hissed.

Frosch felt a cold chill and deathly sweat began to appear on his forehead. Then he looked around. There in the workshop stood a thousand coffins. Frosch woke up and never went back to sleep the rest of that strange night.

By that time, Boniface Strumm was also wide awake.

He had dreamed that he was laboring in his famous workshop. He was working on one thousand beautiful and lavish uniforms. One thousand uniforms fit to embellish the noblest of dukes. Oh how wonderfully noisy it was at Strumm's factory! The job had to be finished by midnight. And the job would be finished by midnight. Strumm's workshop never missed a deadline. He would rather pay his employees a special bonus to give them the incentive to work harder and finish on time.

And behold, Boniface Strumm's punctuality was realized again. Once he set a deadline, he would honor it! As soon as midnight came, the alderman victoriously looked around his workshop. He began to count the uniforms until he could count no more. He then burst into a joyful, self-gratifying laughter.

But Boniface Strumm was not laughing alone, and it wasn't his journeymen who were laughing with him. They were lingering about, tired and pale from all the work they had done. Boniface Strumm stood face to face with the Ratcatcher. He sensed a feeling similar to that of despair, but it would be ridiculous for an alderman of Hamelin to fear a wandering ratcatcher.

"I promised you a special bonus and so I give you a special bonus," Strumm almost forced himself to say to his journeymen. "Who could ever claim that I have not kept my word?"

However, the Ratcatcher continued to laugh and it seemed like Satan himself was laughing.

Strumm did not believe much in God. He never saw God in himself or in others. He was more willing to believe in Satan. To Strumm, Satan was more likely to exist.

Yet Strumm managed to gather all his strength. He raised his eyes and looked at the Ratcatcher. He expressed all the pride of that moment in three words:

"One thousand uniforms," he said.

The Ratcatcher stared at the tailor with a silent mockery that shattered what remained of Strumm's pride. The alderman made one last attempt to resist.

"One thousand uniforms," he repeated. "All finished on time."

The Ratcatcher burst into a terrifying and crushing laughter.

"One thousand rags," he hissed.

Strumm instinctively looked around and insane anguish constricted his throat.

One thousand uniforms had turned into a thousand rags. In the midst of this terrifying spectacle, he recognized an image of his own pale face—the face of Boniface Strumm—and this other Strumm suddenly shouted in his own voice Hamelin's famous statement,

"May God help us."

Boniface Strumm did not sleep the rest of that night either.

XI

Even the Ratcatcher had little sleep that night.

Agnes fell asleep embraced by love but an inexplicable anxiety kept the Ratcatcher awake. Perhaps he thought that someone would rob him blind if he fell asleep. But who would possibly want to rob the Ratcatcher? Nevertheless, the Ratcatcher listened as if he suddenly heard someone walking, but it was nothing more than the rhythm of a woman's breathing in her sleep.

The darkness was fading and the first rays of dawn were approaching rather early—it was the month of May.

The Ratcatcher greeted the sunlight, for it brought Agnes back to him. He leaned against the edge of her bed and began watching her. She was sleeping the way fair-minded people sleep—with peace and innocence. Her thin, fragile, and pure body lay with a vulnerability that was intoxicating.

The Ratcatcher stared into her face, revealed by the morning light. It was almost childlike. The moment her eyes closed something shy and gentle would appear. What sort of enigma allowed this woman to change back into a virgin? While he watched her sleep, the Ratcatcher forgot all their recent love making. By that time he could swear that he had never even touched her.

An unusual gentleness never felt before suddenly poured into his calloused heart. The Ratcatcher held his breath and sat without moving a muscle. He feared that Agnes would awaken and rob him of this morning magic. She was dreaming. What was she dreaming about? A doll? Child's play? Butterflies that fly away?

The Ratcatcher was overwhelmed by anguish.

Agnes had never seemed so beautiful to him. Never before did he realize how easily the beauty of a woman could incite him and then disappear. Give a little, take a little, and suddenly there is no trace of magic or grace. The Ratcatcher was capable of many things. He could rid a town of both rats and people but he could not stop time.

Agnes slept, and for a moment the Ratcatcher wished to wake her with kisses and rid himself of his anxiety. But then he began to fear his own wish, for he too would rob this sleeping creature of something.

That night was strange, but so was the morning. The Ratcatcher leaned over that fragile body he dared not touch in the morning light. The restlessness in his vagrant heart began to grow. Who would come to rob him of his love? When would he do it? From where would he come? The Ratcatcher traveled through many towns and countries. He traveled to these places so that others would submit to him, but he himself would remain free.

It was only during this past night that he felt something anchoring him. He left towns, he abandoned countries, and his desires never led him to feel nostalgic. He never looked back but always ahead. He realized that this time he would not leave Hamelin in this fashion.

The thought that he would allow himself to be tied down seemed laughable and absurd. However, this strain of thinking kept revisiting him. Finally, it seemed neither laughable nor absurd.

The Ratcatcher felt strange. His heart grew heavy, as if it carried the sorrow of thousands, and then it felt light, as if it carried all their happiness as well.

His eyes were wide open. That morning the world was reborn. Yesterday held joy and pain. But yesterday's joy was a shadow of today's joy and yesterday's pain was a shadow of today's pain. Once as a boy, the Ratcatcher had stood by the sea. A ship passed with its sails billowing in the wind. The boy suddenly was overcome by the desire to praise this journey regardless of its outcome. *Greetings, Fair Ship, and those who sail upon it! And good luck to you who might shipwreck!*

As a boy the Ratcatcher shouted these words to challenge destiny. They revisited him as a man, but it was a long-delayed echo that was much more powerful than the original shout.

The Ratcatcher's anxiety became unbearable. The blood in his veins was pounding. His body demanded motion and action. He quietly slipped out of bed, but his movement managed to wake the sleeping woman. She was only half-awake. She opened her eyes, touched the Ratcatcher's forehead with her hands and said, "Stay."

But that was the one thing the Ratcatcher could not do. He waited a few seconds. Agnes went back to sleep. She closed her eyes, and her hands dropped lifelessly back on the bed.

The Ratcatcher left quietly — ever so quietly. He stepped out into the garden. And what a garden it was! The bushes and flowerbeds were fresh. The trees were releasing an abundance of blossoms onto the path. The Ratcatcher looked at the sky. It was clear, pure, and wider than yesterday. The sun carried the color of dawn as it was giving birth to the day. The Ratcatcher looked at the ground and saw that it was pure and refreshed by the morning dew. His heart too seemed pure and transparent.

Was he truly tied down? Perhaps, but these shackles offered him quite a flight! Oh the heights the Ratcatcher was reaching! The tower at the Holy Trinity Cathedral was tall, but it seemed minuscule compared with the altitude of his flight. Was he truly tied down? Perhaps, but do we not sometimes use such shackles to bind the world together as one?

The early wind knew how to revive a face still hot from a morning bed. Its touch was quite refreshing! The flowers smelled good—a magnitude of flowers of all colors and fragrances. He could pick any one he liked. They were all waiting there for the Ratcatcher. Gently and with a sense of triumph he reached for the most beautiful flower, but his anxiety prevented him from picking it.

He looked around once more. The world was beautiful! And behold, behind the town of Hamelin, Koppel Mountain reappeared. The mountain was high, much higher than the Holy Trinity, but even it could not compete with the altitude of the Ratcatcher's flight. There were even higher and higher mountains. He already had seen many of them and there were still many to conquer, yet none of them could exceed the level of his flight.

It was a beautiful world and it was wonderful to be in it with such a magical musical instrument capable of anything. The Pope had power, but what was the power of the Pope compared with that of the Ratcatcher? The emperor had power but how could he stand up to the melodies produced by the Ratcatcher? The Ratcatcher was trying to deceive the restlessness of his soul, but it was impossible to deceive himself. His eyes opened wide and he suddenly caught a glimpse of a dark speck among so many clear and magical things. It was small but as it kept coming closer, it grew larger. There was nothing special about this dark speck; it was just a man.

There was nothing special about this man either. His walk was neither too hasty nor too slow. The citizens of Hamelin never relished haste. However, they were accustomed to arriving on time. This person was certainly a citizen of Hamelin.

The Ratcatcher had never met this man and did not know him personally. He never wanted to meet or know him. He wanted to meet him least of all that particularly strange morning. But the man was coming closer, at a steady pace. He was someone who had a destination. The Ratcatcher's heart was still heavy, as if it carried the sorrow of thousands, but the lightness that carried joy suddenly vanished. Every child in Hamelin could name the approaching man, for every child in town knew Tall Kristian.

XII

They stood across from each other. Kristian gave the Ratcatcher a scowl. His suspicious eyes were looking for something they could hold on to but the Ratcatcher easily avoided his stone-cold look. Kristian clenched his fist instinctively. The Ratcatcher did not change his expression. He was waiting. Kristian was searching for words and his anger grew when he could not find them.

Kristian glanced at the Ratcatcher and then at Agnes's front door. His spiteful eyes seemed to be measuring the distance between the two and their proximity gave him the incentive to speak.

"I know you. You're the Ratcatcher."

The Ratcatcher bowed his head and said nothing. Kristian's tone was sarcastic but that was to no avail. Not a single feature on the Ratcatcher's face changed. To the contrary, his eyes were ignited with a light that held Kristian hostage like a warden holds a prisoner. But Kristian did not recognize the terms of his imprisonment and he spoke once more.

"What are you doing here, Ratcatcher? What is it that you want here in Hamelin?"

The Ratcatcher bent down toward a rose bush and he picked the prettiest of roses.

"What am I doing here? As you can see, I am smelling roses."

Kristian's piercing eyes shot out a malicious flame.

"It is not becoming of a ratcatcher to smell flowers. After all, you are a ratcatcher."

"A ratcatcher? Why yes I am—at your service. I drown rats, if you please, or if I myself please. I drowned many rats in Hamelin but today I don't wish to drown any."

"You are in someone else's garden, Ratcatcher."

"I am in a place where I smell rats. The aldermen and you are of the opinion that there are no more rats in Hamelin. You are mistaken and so are the aldermen. They are here and I believe that they are near. I have a good sense for this. After all, it is my trade! I was at the Thirsty Man last night, but don't assume that I was there only because I have the ability to seek out rats, many rats. I must admit, I don't like the Thirsty Man. The innkeeper Röger is overly courteous and his wine is too sour. I am sober now, and I am telling you there are rats in town. They're simply more timid. Before they were annoying, they would dare to jump on a table. But who will guarantee that they won't become annoying once more?"

"It's our problem now, Ratcatcher. We will be able to tame them."

"Only with the help of my fife. I advise you, friend, you should be aware of my fife. Rats die when they listen to it. You should never wish to hear it."

And the Ratcatcher studied the garden in bloom, the house among the flowers as well as Tall Kristian. He then began to leave at a slow and steady pace.

Kristian gazed upon him with a baffled expression. He wanted to say even more. The words were on his lips, but the Ratcatcher was already too far away. Tall Kristian shook his head and went straight for the door.

Agnes was still sleeping. Kristian watched her as the Ratcatcher's words resonated in his head. The image of the sleeping woman became clearer as the Ratcatcher was disappearing farther away into the mist. Agnes slept with an innocent and childlike expression on her face.

XIII

The Ratcatcher walked. His heart was light again. The morning encounter was a cloud that was floating across the sky only to evaporate at a later time. The sky turned clear like never before.

All of the Ratcatcher's natural abilities suddenly seemed to be multiplying. He could see all the way to the mountains and hear the farthest and softest of sounds. He walked as if he had shoes that could cover seven miles in one step. Time passed quickly on his journey. The Ratcatcher was walking but it seemed as if the landscape around him was moving, not the Ratcatcher himself. The walls of Hamelin were too constricting and the streets too narrow. The Ratcatcher was leaving Hamelin. Was he leaving only to return later? He himself did not know. He passed the town gate where a beggar sat. He was old and blind, broken down by old age and sickness. He was sitting there and begging.

The Ratcatcher threw him a coin. The beggar felt the piece and monotonously replied, "Good luck to you, Pilgrim."

And behold, he saw the fields as they were being farmed! Voices of men and women resonating from each parcel, breaching the same fresh and pure air the Ratcatcher was breathing! The voices sounded happy and high-spirited and the Ratcatcher thought that he understood the language of these people.

A bit further along, the Ratcatcher came upon grazing plains where local cows were feeding. As he passed them, they would lift their heads, calmly sounding a contented "moo," and the Ratcatcher thought that he understood the language of animals.

Then he came to the woods. It was at Saint Mary's Preserve, that remarkable and ancient forest that knew all the loves of Hamelin's sons and daughters, their passions and their pains. It knew all the joy and betrayal of love, its sparks and its retreats. It sheltered secret hideouts and sanctuaries for that particular purpose.

There was also a forest on Koppel Mountain. But Koppel's pines seemed rather gloomy compared with these oak trees, especially when they were standing in the midst of a fresh, lively, and tranquil spring morning. It was as if the birds in the old branches and its undergrowth were greeting the new day. And the Ratcatcher thought that he understood the language of birds.

There was, however, a spot in the preserve that was completely quiet. It was where a portrait of St. Mary was once placed to commemorate a crime that had been committed long ago. Someone killed a wealthy merchant on his way from the market. The murderers were never found, but the merchant's widow had a picture of St. Mary placed at the sight of this evil deed. It was odd to see this place remain so sad and silent. If you ever led a dog around there, he would whine and whimper. Birds would always fly past this place, but they would never nest there. At least that is what folks from Hamelin claimed. Nevertheless, one thing was for certain: There wasn't a quieter and more peaceful spot in this forest. Once in a while the wind would blow, followed by the rustle of leaves. And the Ratcatcher thought that he understood the language of leaves.

The greenery suddenly opened up and the river reflected light upon it. Fresher air embraced the Ratcatcher. He was far, far away from town. There was no sign of the Holy Trinity Cathedral. Not even the peak of Koppel Mountain could be seen from this place. The river waves passing by knew nothing of Gottlieb Frosch and Boniface Strumm, though the two were known well both near and far. These waters flowed so quietly and the Ratcatcher thought that he understood the language of water.

The Ratcatcher's thoughts seemed remarkable—as if time and space were speaking to him:

"I am the Past," said one voice.

"I am the Future," said another.

"I was beautiful," said the Past.

"I will be beautiful," said the Future.

"I had it all—laughter, tears, dreams and awakenings," said the Past.

"I will have it all—laughter, tears, dreams and awakenings," said the Future.

And there, between the Future and the Past, behold—a wonderful Present!

On the mountaintop where the Ratcatcher stood, one could see the entire region, an uninhabited and yet promising land. And on the mountaintop where he stood, the Ratcatcher felt how wonderful it was to be alive.

He gazed upon the surface of the river. A boat was floating on it. At first, the Ratcatcher thought the boat was empty, but soon it was apparent that someone was sleeping curled up on its bottom. The waves were carrying the boat and it was floating with the current toward the Ratcatcher's bank. In an instant, the boat hit land.

"Hello there!" called the Ratcatcher.

The sleeping person did not answer.

"Hello there!" the Ratcatcher repeated, and instantaneously the boat hit a tree branch that was reaching above the surface of the river. The impact woke the sleeping person. He stood up and gazed at the Ratcatcher with drowsy eyes.

The Ratcatcher recognized Jörgen. He couldn't say why this poor and insignificant fisherman, who would never harm him, was disturbing his mood.

"You fell asleep," he said.

"I fell asleep," Jörgen said softly with a touch of sorrow. "I thought that the two girls would come back again, but I fell asleep and they never came. Or could I have perhaps slept through their arrival?"

Jörgen's expression was hopelessly comical, but the Ratcatcher did not laugh.

"I will have to head back," the Fisherman said. "It's a long way and I have to row against the current. It'll be a difficult journey and my nets came up empty. I'll have another hungry day."

Jörgen's expression seemed even more pitiful, but the Ratcatcher once again resisted his urge to laugh. He remembered the words he uttered from the night before: "You should allow yourself to have a woman, but never allow her to have you."

XIV

The Ratcatcher headed back to Hamelin. His anxiety had forced him outside the walls of the town, but it dragged him back even more relentlessly. He walked along the bank of the river. It created turns and zigzagged through the forest and meadows and by willow trees.

Children were playing in the woods. They were girls and they carried dolls that were rough and handmade. They nurtured these dolls, embracing them close to their bosoms and gently soothing them with the words "My child."

The Ratcatcher gazed upon the river that carried Jörgen's boat. Workers were scything the grass on the meadows. The fragrance was intoxicating.

"How is your wife doing?" said one worker to the other.

"She is doing well, praise the Lord. She is walking now, everything is back to normal."

"And the child?"

"Healthy," the questioned man responded in a

happy and proud voice. "He is a handsome boy."

The Ratcatcher glanced at the river. Jörgen's boat was running slowly. The current was becoming stronger.

In the thicket on an uprooted willow tree two old men were warming themselves in the sun.

"He was my last child, and he is also dead," the first one said with a sad and tired voice.

"All my children are alive, but it's as if they were dead to me," his companion sighed from the tree stump across from him. He got up from the shade and feverishly looked for the sun that had moved to the side.

The Ratcatcher glanced at the river. Jörgen's boat was nowhere in sight, though the current did calm a bit. Was Jörgen exhausted? Did he give up the struggle?

The Ratcatcher continued to walk. He did not know how long he had been walking but judging by the position of the sun he could recognize that it was late and the day was gradually coming to an end. How long was he going to continue? He didn't know the answer himself. One thing he did know was that he had to hurry before the gate to the city closed for the night.

"Good luck to you, Pilgrim," someone said out of nowhere. The Ratcatcher looked around. Was it the beggar by the town gate? But how could that poor creature make his way to this place when he could barely move from one door to another?

"Good luck to you, Pilgrim," the voice repeated and it sounded tempting and mocking. But this time the Ratcatcher was certain it wasn't the old beggar who was calling. The voice sounded more like it was Tall Kristian's.

The Ratcatcher smiled. Tall Kristian was in his uncle's shop. He would never dare venture outside Hamelin's walls without proper reason. Days were never squandered in Hamelin. So who was it that suddenly spoke to him from behind?

That morning on his way to this place, the Ratcatcher had understood everything—people, animals, birds, leaves, and water. How, then, could he suddenly be hearing nothing but taunting and tempting voices? And why was it making him feel so uneasy? The Ratcatcher could go where he wanted. He could stop where he wanted. He could leave whenever he wanted. Was he then truly bound to this town of Hamelin?

He proudly grabbed his fife. It was certainly there. No one took it from him. He felt safe as long as it was in his possession. He did not lose any of his power.

But the Ratcatcher remained restless. Night was approaching. Would he return in time? Would they close the gates to the city in front of him?

What did these new and binding feelings mean for the Ratcatcher? Was he suddenly obligated to spend the night in Hamelin—in a town that a short while ago had been foreign to him? The Ratcatcher had traveled to many lands and towns, and, when he bid them farewell, not one pulled him back with such an uncontrollable force. The Ratcatcher wanted to rebel, so he did rebel. He decided to sleep outside and he actually lay down in the soft grass. The night was damp and beautiful. He wanted to see the stars and be far away from people. He was lying in the grass, but the ground felt like it was burning from underneath. His anxiety began to escalate and defeat him. He got up. His defeat put on a mask of victory. Could he possibly be afraid of returning to Hamelin? Who could forbid him to come back? He still had unsettled scores to resolve with Frosch and Strumm and all the aldermen, and of course, with Tall Kristian. Why was he suddenly thinking about Tall Kristian? What business did he have with him? Tall Kristian mattered to him about as much as a rock on the side of a road. Why had he returned to the Ratcatcher's thoughts? Why did his thoughts return to the house he had left just this morning? He shouldn't have left the house or he shouldn't be coming back to it. That was clear. In spite of everything, the Ratcatcher was able to think clearly.

The Ratcatcher walked faster and faster. However, his walk was not as light as it had been in the morning. The shoes that took seven-mile steps suddenly disappeared or perhaps lost their power. It seemed that the Ratcatcher was walking like everyone else. He was walking like the aldermen in Hamelin, like Kristian. But then his walk increased to a speed that would be unbecoming of an alderman. Tall Kristian, however, could get away with that pace if he was rushing to attend to a wealthy customer.

But Tall Kristian was not waiting for the Ratcatcher. Perhaps no one was waiting for him. Nevertheless, the Ratcatcher shifted his direction toward the gates of Hamelin. Thankfully, they were still open.

Good luck to you, Pilgrim. For some reason those meaningless words kept haunting the Ratcatcher. They were lashing at him with mockery. But why were they doing this? It was not wise to mock the Ratcatcher. The citizens of Hamelin were mostly sleeping, but they could easily be awakened by something unpleasant. Such were the thoughts of the Ratcatcher as a rumble from behind signaled the closing of the town gate. The Ratcatcher turned around and it was as if a trap door had shut behind him.

XV

Several days had passed since the Ratcatcher's last visit to the Thirsty Man Tavern. The inappropriate comments he had made on his way out had stirred up the patrons. No one ever dared — and many people had come to Röger's place — to utter such arrogant words to the town's aldermen. Only someone from out of town could do such a thing — someone whose origin and past were a mystery and therefore subject to various interpretations.

The following day, news of the Ratcatcher's threats was circling throughout town. On the third day, a rather significant incident occurred. Stazi Dörrick, the Bürgermeister's wife, gave birth to twins and died that same day. The serious and sad event was discussed widely. Though once or twice someone remembered the Ratcatcher, his threats no longer seemed dangerous to anyone. When another day passed and nothing else happened, the anxiety disappeared. And though earlier the fear was impossible to deny, it was certain to the townspeople that yesterday's dangerous threat seemed to be today's rubbish. It was the wine talking instead of the Ratcatcher, wine stored in good Röger's cellar. The Ratcatcher had been drinking from a good vintage.

And then there was the fact that people forget. Memory was very fickle in the town of Hamelin. Yesterday they might have been in love but today no one would know a thing about it. Yesterday they hated each other and today it was a child's fairytale. Yesterday they were afraid and today Boniface Strumm and Gottlieb Frosch were walking calmly beneath the archway of the square.

The Ratcatcher could not explain what pushed him toward the Thirsty Man Tavern, where he had vowed never to return. He went there inadvertently, almost as if he was in a trance. He walked through the sinuous streets where he ignored the tempting voices and passionate whispers. He walked until he came to the square by the Holy Trinity.

On the cathedral, high among the gargoyles was a statue of a devil with a cynical and taunting grimace. His goat-like face leaned over Hamelin looking confident of his purpose. The statue's creator had managed to engrave something demonic into his features. The Ratcatcher would gaze at this tempter every time he walked by. That night, the devil caught his eye once again as he grimaced at the bright, moonlit night. The Ratcatcher thought that he heard malicious laughter. He looked around but he saw no one. Was it the devil himself who was laughing up there?

The Ratcatcher was neither superstitious nor a coward. He looked up above and never lowered his eyes. What was that goat-like face seeking up there? What did his malicious laughter want? The Ratcatcher kept looking up and, though he did not understand this laughter, he did realize that it was hostile. If the devil knew how to laugh way up there, then why couldn't he come down and face the Ratcatcher at his level? Let him find out whether the Ratcatcher was truly afraid of him. The devil continued to laugh and, oddly enough, the Ratcatcher suddenly began to understand his words.

"Go," the devil said.

The Ratcatcher understood. Yes, he wants me to go to the Thirsty Man Tavern. It was this force that was tempting the man with the fife. What was waiting for him there? What pitfalls did the demonic creature from above prepare for him? The Ratcatcher headed for the tavern, regardless of what he would face inside. The laughing continued, and though the Ratcatcher did not see him, he was now certain that it was the devil.

The wind in the streets began to pick up. When

the Ratcatcher passed a garden belonging to Ursula, the widow of Lamp the draper, he noticed that all the flowers were shivering from the cold. And though the wind was intrusive and unpleasant, the Ratcatcher didn't shake one bit.

Viktor Dyk

XVI

The Thirsty Man Tavern was deserted because of a stranger who had come in wearing the black robe of a master regent with a chain around his neck—a stranger whose name none of the locals recognized. Immediately after this man arrived, some of the patrons began to feel odd. They were uneasy and claimed that the stranger smelled of sulfur. The patrons, one by one, slowly began to get up and leave while casting dirty looks upon the newcomer. The last of the patrons left shortly before the Ratcatcher entered the tavern. It was not a pleasant moment for the innkeeper, but he did not have the courage to intervene. By then, it was too late and nothing could be salvaged; however, plenty of damage could still be done. It was such thinking that forced Röger to err on the side of caution.

But Röger did not fail to hide his displeasure. He paced almost peevishly across the dining room wearing a frown. It was only when he approached the table where the stranger lingered that he forced a stern and begrudging smile on his face. Black Liza was

72

the only one who remained happy, and her liveliness increased as the tavern emptied of patrons. She clung to the possibility that she could be sent home early to be with her lover.

When the Ratcatcher entered, he stopped at the threshold and looked around. Without realizing how strange his behavior might be, he walked through the entire dining room and sat at the table with the stranger who, until then, had been sitting alone.

They both measured one another with their glances.

The man in the regent master's black robe had a gaunt and pale face with a long, dark beard. He had a restless and inquisitive look in his eyes. One moment he seemed to want to ask many questions. The next, he was concealing everything, as if he suddenly wanted to evaporate and escape. Who was he running from? From what did he want to escape? Black Liza and innkeeper Röger were both trying to eavesdrop. Perhaps they would finally learn something about their mysterious and unwanted guest.

The stranger stared at the Ratcatcher with the look of a man who had just met a long-lost acquaintance. He looked at him as if their meeting was destined.

"You're the Ratcatcher," he said.

"Yes," said the man addressed. He sensed that the stranger was a messenger from the one perched on the cathedral.

"I have been waiting for you."

"Who told you that I would be coming?" The Ratcatcher asked the question but he was well aware what the answer would be.

"He did," the man in the black regent master's robe replied, as he lowered his voice a bit to prevent Black Liza and Röger from eavesdropping. Then he burst into quiet and muffled laughter. A flame erupted in his eyes. It was then that the Ratcatcher noticed that the man's eyes were wide open, though moments before he wouldn't stop squinting.

"He?" the Ratcatcher repeated. "And what does *he* want?"

"He knows much," the stranger whispered. "He is capable of many things."

"Who are you, Stranger, and what do you want from me?" the Ratcatcher asked wistfully.

The man in the black robe smiled once more.

"I am Master Regent Faustus from Wittenberg, the man whom *he* serves."[5]

"And what do you need from me, Master Regent?"

"We are brothers, Ratcatcher. I came to offer you a hand."

---

5 *Translator's note:* According to legend Faust gave his soul to the devil in exchange for the devil's servitude.

"The Ratcatcher has no brothers, the Ratcatcher is alone. He does not need anyone."

"You say such words and yet you deceive yourself as well as others. You need him. He is capable of many things — more than you can imagine. Would you like me to demonstrate?"

The Master Regent beckoned the innkeeper to bring new bottles. When the deed was done, he filled his glass to the brim and emptied it in one gulp. His pale face flushed with the color of wine and agitation.

"Would you believe that I was in Wittenberg only an hour ago?"

"Perhaps I would."

"There are no borders for me, nothing is impossible."

"With his help?"

"Yes."

"For what purpose does he serve you?"

"I can see that we will have an understanding, Ratcatcher. I will tell you all you wish to know. Are you searching for the truth, my friend? Do you strive for knowledge?"

"I drown rats, Master Regent. That is my calling."

"You were created for something greater than merely drowning rats. That is not enough, Ratcatcher. You crave more."

"I love Agnes."

"To love is no better than merely drowning rats. You want more and I will tell you what is necessary. In Wittenberg they say that I sold my soul to the devil. Don't believe it. First of all there is no such thing as a soul. That is what I, Master Regent Faustus of Wittenberg, declare! But the heart exists and I sold my heart."

A new kind of suppressed laughter emanated from the Ratcatcher's restless core.

"I'm not here to buy or sell anything," the Ratcatcher erupted. "There is nothing I need. I am strong."

"You deceive yourself, Ratcatcher. Surely you know by now that you have been deceiving yourself. I used to think like you and so many times I have been wrong! Oh, the amount of time and strength I have wasted! Strength can be restored, but time will never return. And now? Now everything is simple and easy. It didn't cost me much. Just a heart. The heart is a small and insignificant thing. People, however, die because of insignificant things. You have your fife, Ratcatcher. The things you could do with your fife! You could be master of life and death. You can soothe and you can annihilate. You doubt me? Should I show you what he could do? Should I show you what I could do?"

The Master Regent pointed at a lazy, well-fed tomcat that was purring in front of the fireplace.

"Do you see that cat? Would you like me to turn him into a tiger?"

"Please do," the Ratcatcher replied with a smile on his face.

The Master Regent mumbled incomprehensible words and made a strange motion indicating a cross that ended with a ridiculous gesture bordering on blasphemy. Then, suddenly, with an expression of confidence, he crossed his arms on his chest.

"Well then, take a look."

The Ratcatcher fixed his eyes on the tomcat, purring calmly next to the fireplace just as before. Then he looked upon the Master Regent, whose eyes were filled with terror and pride. Without a doubt, to him the tomcat was a tiger that was ready to pounce, but it was only tamed by the Master Regent's powerful stare. The Master Regent took the Ratcatcher by the hand and reassuringly whispered.

"He is terrifying, but do not fear him. You, he will not harm."

The master hesitated for two, three seconds. He wanted to feed on his own fear. Then once again he spoke some incomprehensible word and repeated his spellbinding motions. He then inquisitively turned to the Ratcatcher.

"Do you believe me now?

The Ratcatcher shook his head.

"Is this not enough for you? I will show you more. Would you care to see a palace of Caliphs? Would you like to see the Alhambra?"

Once again the Master Regent whispered and gesticulated, and once more his eyes were filled with amazement at the things he saw. But the Ratcatcher never saw the Alhambra, which seemed so clear to the master. All he saw were the round oak tables in Röger's tavern.

The gaze of intense anticipation that the Master Regent bestowed upon the Ratcatcher suddenly changed into a look of disappointment. He could not understand why his companion continued to disbelieve him.

"Still not convinced? Still not enough?"

The Master Regent thought for a moment.

"I will thus do more," he said. He looked at Black Liza, who was giggling at the strange gestures of the unknown guest.

"Behold that woman. She is rough, foul, and deplorable. Would you like for me to turn her into Helen, for whom the Trojans and Achaeans murdered? Would you like me to cleanse the grime of orgies and the abomination of sin from this woman? I can accomplish that."

The Ratcatcher remained silent.

The Master Regent repeated his experiment. Once again he mumbled his formula and stared at Black Liza, who was sprawled with raucous laughter. But her laughter did not confuse the Master Regent. He raised his hand as if he wished to bless her but stopped short of doing so.

"Behold, here she is."

When the Ratcatcher heard the Master Regent's delighted words, he looked at him. Without a doubt, the Master Regent saw something precious and beautiful. He was completely enamored and infatuated. His eyes could not separate from a certain point and his shoulders expanded as if he wanted to embrace this emptiness. There was no doubt this was all a fairytale to him. It was magic, a miracle — an unbelievable and enormous miracle. And the Ratcatcher almost allowed himself to gaze upon the individual who was supposed to be Helen with a sense of fear. But it was only Black Liza who stood in the doorway. She was too real — the way all of Hamelin knew her. The way all her lovers knew her. Her laughter was loud and rough. The Master Regent's motions and the sublime look in his eyes were obviously amusing her.

"That is Helen," the Master whispered dreamingly. "That is her. She is beautiful. Oh, how beautiful she is!"

His expanding shoulders wanted to embrace this unbelievable miracle, but they embraced only emptiness. However, that did not dispel the Master Regent's desire. His arms fiercely and feverishly embraced something invisible.

The Ratcatcher, a friend of things clear and certain, felt anguish, as if he stood on precarious and loose soil that was always treacherously caving in to his weight. His hands touched the table. It was sturdy. His hands touched his glass. It too was sturdy. He stood up and the cold stone underneath his feet was sturdy.

The Master Regent took another moment to indulge in his rather unique reality. Then, almost forcefully, he detached himself from it. He uttered his little formula and made his little motion. He was more exhausted than at peace.

It was only after another glass of wine that the Master Regent, who gazed at his table companion victoriously, suddenly revitalized. But the Master Regent noticed neither a sense of euphoria nor belief from his companion. He stared at the Ratcatcher with a strange and disappointed look.

"You still don't believe?"

"No."

"Did you see what I saw?"

"No."

The Master Regent grew sad.

"Your heart is what is stopping you, friend. A man who ponders too much should never have a heart. You will see that your heart will be your demise. What a waste. What a waste of your fife. It was made to do greater things. You are my brother. You are more than a natal brother. I pity you."

"As I pity you," the Ratcatcher replied calmly and without mockery. But once he uttered those words, Master Regent Faustus of Wittenberg vanished. The Ratcatcher sat at the round table alone. Other than a sleepy innkeeper and a laughing Black Liza, no one was in the dining room.

Röger was leaning against a pillar. He was frightened and alarmed by the events that had just occurred. Black Liza, confused by the stranger's sudden disappearance, no longer laughed.

"Did you see that?" Röger asked.

The Ratcatcher silently nodded.

"He disappeared! Everything else is here but him. There have been some odd people visiting Hamelin lately."

The Ratcatcher was able to sense the insult from the innkeeper's words but he didn't respond. He was too focused on the Master Regent's disappearance. The Ratcatcher's silence could not calm the innkeeper. The vanishing bothered him for more serious reasons.

"I would like to know if you will at least pay for your tab. As God is my witness, that Master Regent was not a man who drank lightly. And if he did not pay..."

But the innkeeper's fears were unfounded. He hurried to the table where the Ratcatcher now sat alone. A golden coin lay in the place where, a few moments ago, Master Regent Faustus of Wittenberg had been sitting. Röger was still uneasy. He took the coin into his hand and checked its authenticity.

He must have felt satisfied about its value because he calmly and almost cheerfully stated, "This coin most likely came from the devil's mint, but you can buy more for a devil's quid than for an angel's groat."[6]

The Ratcatcher paid his tab and slowly began to leave.

A sharp wind blew through the streets and lashed the Ratcatcher's face. When he passed the Holy Trinity Cathedral, he looked up to where he had heard the devil's laughter earlier. And there he was, leaning over the town of Hamelin, and it was still possible to hear his laughter and his malicious and mocking words: "Go! Go further, Ratcatcher!"

---

6 *Translator's note*: A *groat* is a silver coin, also known as a *Groschen* which was common currency throughout the Holy Roman Empire.

XVII

She stood at the door as she once had when the Ratcatcher, with a light mind and heart, first entered Hamelin. But she was not smiling. Her eyes gazed sternly and feverishly into the night's darkness. She seemed to be standing there awaiting her destiny rather than her happiness. She stood nailed to her door like a cross.

The Ratcatcher's quiet steps were moving closer to her. This time a burning desire was not quivering in Agnes's body the way it did many times before. She was simply submitting more passively to an unknown desire. Her eyes were not burning with anticipation. They seemed sunken without hope and a belief that the night might ever retreat. But the Ratcatcher did not notice this. All that he saw was the white figure in the doorway and then he picked up his pace. His desire, in its entirety, raced toward Agnes. He forgot everything in this desire — the aldermen's treachery and broken promises, the pale wizard who couldn't conjure a thing, the one who was laughing high above on the Holy Trinity Cathedral. Doctor Faustus was far away from there. Even the devil was far away in that moment. What could the Ratcatcher possibly look for in this quiet and remote home which sheltered his love?

The Ratcatcher walked. He walked with his eyes closed. He could do this with ease, for he knew his path well. He opened his arms in the right moment to embrace her fully blossomed and warm body. Just yesterday and the night before she was kissing him with passionate lips on his closed eyelids, and her bare shoulders pressed upon his neck.

At the right moment he opened his arms, but something strange happened. The body he embraced did not resist, but it didn't show signs of life; it showed signs of a cold and troublesome fading life. He did not feel hot kisses. He did not hear whispers of love and passion.

"Agnes!" erupted from the Ratcatcher's lips. But his words could not chase away her demons.

"Ratcatcher," whispered the one he embraced, but her voice sounded like it came from such an unapproachable distance that the Ratcatcher could barely hear it. It was just a word, not an answer.

It was time for the Ratcatcher to open his eyes in the same way he opened his arms. There was no doubt that in this moonlit night near the doorway he was embracing the woman he loved. But her face was pale, almost livid. The Ratcatcher would have loved to think that this was due to the reflection of the moonlight, but then suddenly it seemed as if he heard laughter in the distance.

The devil, who was tempting the Ratcatcher, had slowly descended from the tower on the Holy Trinity. Taking cunning steps, he followed closely behind the Ratcatcher to this remote corner. His muffled laughter came from behind the blossoms of an elderberry bush in the garden. Other than the laughter, there was silence. But the Ratcatcher understood the languages of both silence and laughter. He knew he had to ask her. He also knew he would receive a cruel answer.

But the Ratcatcher was no coward and so he decided to ask this dangerous question.

"What troubles you, Agnes?"

The Ratcatcher's voice was quiet and soothing. Only his voice could sound that way. His hands softly touched the helpless and sad body of his lover. Agnes's eyes were wide open and there was something infinitely plain and baffled in them. She was not trying to escape because there was nowhere to go. She did not defend herself because there was no way she could. Her hopeless eyes, resigned to her fate, caused the Ratcatcher pain. He embraced Agnes even more forcefully, as forcefully as the first time they met. But there was something different now. The pain was still present, but the passion had disappeared.

"Surely you can talk to me, Agnes," the Ratcatcher insisted. "Tell me what ails you. Your silence is more painful than anything you could possibly say."

But the Ratcatcher wished he could take back those last words. Did he mean what he had just said?

Agnes made a heavy and weak motion like someone who was gaining consciousness.

"Come," she whispered sadly. It was obvious she was submitting to him and with the fatalism that only a weak woman could possess, she allowed herself to be consumed by a fierce and violent current. Where would this current take her?

They walked. This route was also familiar to the Ratcatcher when he traveled it in the darkness. Nevertheless, he managed to stumble and, as he stumbled, he thought of Tall Kristian. Oddly, there was no sign of Kristian. The Ratcatcher usually did not feel jealous. Kristian seemed harmless and shallow to him—someone who wasn't worth his time. But at that particular moment the thought of his rival severely wounded the Ratcatcher's pride. He leaned toward Agnes who was walking in front of him in the darkness.

She felt his hot breath as he asked,

"Is it Kristian?"

She did not answer. They both continued walking silently through the darkness and even though they both knew this darkness well from past nights, it suddenly seemed unfamiliar.

The clock on the tower struck the hour. This monotonous sound carried the Ratcatcher into a state of delirium for a few seconds. But then he was awakened by the inconsolable lament that Agnes let out. Agnes, who used to laugh into the spring night.

"My God!"

XVIII

A chilling silence followed her lament.

The Ratcatcher carried Agnes to a bed that was close by. She would never have been able to make it there on her own. She was drained of all her strength. The Ratcatcher leaned over her pale body and waited in vain for her word, an explanation or confession.

Nothing followed. The seconds were brutally long. Agnes was not gaining consciousness. Her breathing was faint and could barely be heard. In this quiet evening the Ratcatcher could feel the pulse of his own vagrant heart.

He continued to wait.

Night fell over Hamelin. Everyone rested between old and new pettiness, old and new sin, and old and new poverty. Everyone was being lulled by homely and minuscule happiness, which wasn't truly happiness at all. Everyone except the Ratcatcher and perhaps Sepp Jörgen, who was lost in his helpless desires.

Sepp Jörgen too was as broken and pitiful as Agnes. And yet, at that moment his misfortune seemed only faint and small.

Night fell over Hamelin. Many different nights had fallen over Hamelin before. The Ratcatcher remembered one night in particular: it was the same one that Strumm and Frosch found so unrestful. The night that the Ratcatcher himself could not sleep. Again and again his mind felt his memories intrude.

Suddenly, Agnes gained consciousness. What time was it? The Ratcatcher did not know. Everything seemed an eternity to him — a desperate and cruel eternity. Her hand began searching for his. The Ratcatcher leaned over Agnes. In the moonlight her paleness seemed intensified and that terrified the Ratcatcher. Their eyes met. He looked at her seriously and inquisitively, but he did not find fear in her eyes — only sadness.

And then deep within her throat, a place where words had been dying for such a long time, words suddenly began to flow — yet they were all the more hurtful because she was not reproaching the Ratcatcher.

"It happened. I could not help it. I do not love him. I can feel that I don't love him and it still happened."

And feeble Agnes suddenly gained enough strength to let out a fierce and passionate scream.

"Kill me! Kill me now! I don't want his child! I don't want it! I don't!"

She sat up halfway on her bed and clenched on

to the Ratcatcher's arm as if she were drowning. The Ratcatcher stood motionless as he took in Agnes's cruel words. He stood there like a statue, an apparition. But his heart was scorched by the chill of a single second. All that was left was cruel pain.

"Kill me!" Agnes repeated.

She collapsed back on her bed and lay there passively with the beaten eyes of someone who had been unsuccessfully searching a long time, but no longer had the strength to further her quest.

The Ratcatcher leaned over Agnes. He was sullen and motionless. He wanted to say something but he couldn't. He wanted to leave, but he wasn't able. He wanted to look elsewhere, but he was incapable of climbing out of this rift of despair.

It was a strange moment. He suddenly had a vision of making an incredible flight. But it differed from the flight of that one morning he last encountered Tall Kristian.

His whole life thundered around him yet somewhere away from him. Distant voices were calling upon him. Goblets were ringing with one toast after another. He heard laughter and happiness. Bells were ringing as if it were a holiday. And then there was the silence, terrible silence.

Landscapes were passing by in front of the

Ratcatcher's eyes. They surpassed each other with their beauty. They had the joyous appeal of the south and the stern beauty of the north. The rivers flowed. The mountains reached to their tallest heights. The towns rumbled and oceans roared. And then there was emptiness — terrible emptiness.

Faces of women passed by the Ratcatcher's eyes — women with pale and swarthy complexions, women of many races and origins. They passed and whispered gentleness and love. They passed and nodded a greeting. And then there was nightfall.

An extraordinary and chaotic flight!

Everything suddenly disappeared and the Ratcatcher ceased to feel. All these women left and the Ratcatcher had no regrets. His proud and fierce heart traveled far, far away to new horizons where he would never settle down — where he would travel on.

Agnes! Agnes! What was it about Agnes that attracted the Ratcatcher? There were more beautiful women. There were more intoxicating women.

Is one bound to another more by pain or by passion?

Agnes's eyes gazed helplessly forward. She was resigned to her fate. She no longer repeated "Kill me," but her expressions rendered no happiness or hope — only pain.

The pain was silent. And Agnes's body was cold

and motionless, like the body of a woman who was beaten to death.

The Ratcatcher stood over Agnes. Mountains were crumbling upon his heart. His memories were so heavy. Seconds were extremely long, but they still passed. The sun began to rise and the Ratcatcher was still remembering his earlier departure and his meeting with Tall Kristian by the garden gate early that morning.

Was it not true that he left in order to make room for this other man?

The Ratcatcher tried to gather his thoughts and forcefully overpower his heart's resistance.

One thing was certain: It was necessary for him to leave Hamelin. His heart would reclaim its freedom once he was beyond the town walls. The birds sing joyously on the road for those who journey through the shadows of old oak trees and the heat of the loanins.[7] Many beautiful and extraordinary things would await and welcome him. The Ratcatcher had seen many things, yet he had not seen everything in the world. Why should we remember pain that has passed? Why should we remember a doorway that was already shut behind us?

---

7 *Translator's note: A loanin* is a path or opening between two cultivated fields.

Should he leave Hamelin?

But his memories took him to that recent day when he was abandoning Hamelin, an act that seemed to cater to Tall Kristian's desires. The Ratcatcher assumed that he was leaving a free man but he returned bound by an unclear desire, one that grew constantly more powerful and cruel. It was impelling him to return to those repulsive walls, to that heinous town—that town of minuscule lives and minuscule hearts where the Ratcatcher's love had settled. Surely it was now possible to abandon Hamelin through its gates. But where would the Ratcatcher go? How long could he succeed in escaping his memories?

Should he stay? How could he possibly?

He could no longer stand to look at Agnes. He could no longer stand to look at Tall Kristian. He could no longer live next to that man. And what about the Ratcatcher himself? What could he do in a town where he had so carelessly eliminated all the rats far too quickly? What sort of ratcatcher was he—unfree and chained by an inexplicable set of shackles?

But what option did he have if he could neither stay nor leave Hamelin?

Agnes stared at the Ratcatcher with her resigned eyes. She was reading his thoughts and his heart.

She did not expect anything. All she wanted was to

continue to gaze at his dear and sullen face.

"Go," she said quietly with sadness.

He refused, shaking his head, but Agnes stubbornly insisted. She was begging for his departure as much as for his forgiveness.

"Go, Ratcatcher. Go anywhere. Forget me..." And at that moment her voice sounded soft and quiet, like music fading away, "I can no longer go on, Ratcatcher."

"I will not leave," the Ratcatcher howled. "It is futile to leave when I would only want to return."

"You will not return, Ratcatcher."

She tried to smile, which only saddened the Ratcatcher. There was nothing to say that would lighten the moment. She was carrying a heavy burden. But how do you lessen the load of such a burdened soul?

"Go, Ratcatcher," Agnes insisted once again. "I'm tired. I am deathly tired."

The low arches of the room's ceiling were closing in on the Ratcatcher. He wanted to break something fiercely. He wanted to scream and beat someone but there was no one. Agnes continued to insist.

"I am leaving then," the Ratcatcher said. "But I will return."

"Then you will return," Agnes replied quietly. "Until we meet again, Ratcatcher."

She squeezed his hand without saying a word.

He left. Agnes kept watching him from behind long after he had gone.

Perhaps the Ratcatcher would never have left, had he seen the look in her eyes.

XIX

"You are sad, Agnes," her mother said.

Agnes neither smiled nor uttered a single word that whole day. Her sorrow brought back a spark of compassion to her mother's weary heart.

"It's nothing," Agnes said soothingly. Attempting to sound lighthearted, she asked, "Do you know what I miss? I would like to hear a fairy tale."

Mother looked stunned. She did not expect such a request from her grown daughter's lips.

"You used to tell me fairy tales. It was so long ago. I miss that."

"Who knows whether I have forgotten them all by now," her mother replied.

"So many fairy tales! One was about Koppel Mountain. You must still know that one."

"No I don't."

"Tell me the one about Koppel Mountain and the land of the Seven Castles. Tell me that fairy tale."

Mothers had told the tale of Koppel Mountain and the land of Seven Castles to children in Hamelin since the beginning of time. It rendered Koppel's peak more mysterious and tempting. The fairy tale told the story of the seven castles that surrounded a beautiful valley unparalleled by anything in the world. Seven castles with seven gates protected the valley. At each gate stood a knight in full armor guarding everyone inside from pain and sorrow. The people in this land were kind and would never hurt one another. One would never find sin or guilt in this land. The sky was pure and clear. Oh how beautiful it was to live in the land of Seven Castles! If the children of Hamelin wished to enter this earthly Eden, it was simple—all they had to do was climb Koppel Mountain. The gateway to the land of Seven Castles lay at the abyss. They would have to journey there through darkness and night, enduring sad and reproachful voices. If they succeeded through these obstacles, they would then find delight and bliss.

Agnes knew all this and had heard it before. She remembered all of it at that moment.

"Do you still remember the song about the Seven Castles? How does it go?"

Her mother nodded and began to sing in a feeble and trembling voice.

Seven Castles in this land
Where dreams of beauty vigil keep,

Viktor Dyk

Where gently in its soothing span
The day awakes the ones who sleep.
Seven Castles in this place
Calm the sadness between their walls,
And those who carry joy and grace
Are the strongest of them all.
Pain and treachery — as well as guilt —
Fear the knights who guard this ground,
In the shadows of these castles built
No pain and sorrow can be found...

Agnes's mother grew tired, so Agnes therefore continued with the song:

This land of Seven Castles
Is as beautiful as sin,
Where the sounds of wailing forests
Cannot drown the mirth within.
It is a land full of light,
A world of renowned fame.
Where flowers sing with pure delight
Like choristers in a sea of grain.
This land, it heals the human heart
With hopes and dreams and soothing hands
Give us, dear Lord, here at the start
The strength to reach this joyous land.

Those final words sounded endearing and passionate as they came from Agnes's lips. Her mother instinctively clasped her gaunt and dry hands. The old woman leaned her head forward and began to think.

Agnes approached the pensive woman.

"Is there any truth to this fairy tale, Mother? And if there isn't, do we have any other choice than to believe it anyway? Farewell, Mother. I'm going for a walk. It's beautiful and clear outside."

"And if Kristian stops by?"

"He can wait."

"And what if the Ratcatcher comes?"

"Tell him to follow me," she said. And then she added pensively, "I'm going to Koppel Mountain."

Her mother seemed disturbed as she stood up.

"Be careful, Agnes. Promise me that you'll be careful."

"I will, Mother."

And Agnes left. She looked at her mother in the doorway and waved farewell back to her. She sang the last two lines of the song once more:

Give us, dear Lord, here at the start
The strength to reach this joyous land.

XX

The river is, at times, like a friend that calms and comforts a person. Its waves flow lightly and its surface seems only slightly darkened. By its banks little fish swim through the clear water. You can reach down and feel the bottom. Then suddenly the water loses its clarity, but not its silence.

The river's waves flow so lightly. They cradle a fisherman in a boat. Travelers sing happy songs, lovers float downward happily and quietly. And if you are tired by the day, if the sun is too cruel or the road too dusty, behold how patiently the waters of the river await you.

The river gives everything. Fish to the fishermen, peace to the soul, cleanliness to the body. But at times the river can be like an enemy or a willful murderer. Suddenly it reaches out of its bank and floods the countryside, ripping out roofs and homes. It rips out soil and life. It insatiably grabs onto anything it can devour. It will carry away tree trunks. It will steal a cradle. It can also take away a child. Far away, so far away it will carry its prey—to other rivers, to the sea.

But then the river will calm itself and once again its waves will flow gently.

Agnes approached the river with weary and hesitating steps. She was sad and silent. She sat on the bank and began to study the current. The water passed and whispered intimate and soothing words in response to the sorrow she expressed upon the bank. And it was as if her dark shadow, not Agnes herself, suddenly rose in a moment of decisiveness. It was where the river was the deepest that she threw herself into the soothing current. She threw herself into the waves so that the stream's humming would drown the sound of her pain. And the waves continued to hum and flow. The water splashed and beat upon the banks. And then there was silence. The river became soothing again.

XXI

Tall Kristian was happily rubbing his hands as he walked back and forth in the room.

He had just returned to the jeweler Berndt's home, where he lived, after visiting his uncle's place. His uncle was seriously ill. He had had a fever for three days. Maid Gertrude sent for a priest. Once his uncle recognized the friar, spiritual solace did not return to him a sense of ease. At times he seemed delirious, other times he wanted to get up and visit the Thirsty Man Tavern. At certain moments he spoke about women and roses; during other moments he began to confess his sins. And they were quite the sins!

Tall Kristian was cheerful. His inheritance was at his fingertips. His future seemed tempting and rosy. Uncle Andreas's heir would not just be anyone. Hamelin would see what Kristian would do with his inheritance. Agnes was his. The future belonged to him.

The door suddenly burst open and interrupted his beautiful dreams. Agnes's mother entered. She was like a phantom, like a ghost. Usually, her quiet and timid steps would silently reveal her presence. But the woman who entered that day was searching for something. Her whole life had vanished from her pale cheeks into her eyes. Behold, the eyes of a mother!

She had been searching for some time to no avail. She first asked her neighbors. Had they seen Agnes? She journeyed through the streets of Hamelin, stopping people who were passing. They brushed her off rudely and answered her evasively. They had seen Agnes, but they could not remember exactly where or when. They saw her pass by, but they could not remember if it was that day or the day before. The citizens of Hamelin had other worries than to pay attention to the whereabouts of one girl. Agnes's mother hung her head and continued to search.

"Have you seen Agnes? Have you seen my child?"

All they could tell her was that Agnes went to the river. Kristian lived on a street close to the river. Did he perhaps know what happened to her? Oh those eyes! Oh those unsettling and inquisitive eyes! They were fixed on Kristian like a condemned man was fixed on hope for leniency. Her lips, trembling from her unsaid words, pled with him silently. Kristian approached her and tried to comfort her. But even he understood that it was dangerous to comfort an unknown pain.

"What happened?" he asked anxiously.

And the mother finally uttered her only words, a single sentence.

"Have you seen Agnes, my child?"

Kristian grew frightened. The Ratcatcher's shadow had risen and begun to scare him. He remembered Agnes's restlessness, her inexplicable sadness and evasive answers.

"Has the Ratcatcher bedeviled her? No, that couldn't be," Kristian would say to himself.

"What has happened to Agnes?" he asked, gasping for breath, "I know nothing of her whereabouts. Tell me what happened?"

He never received an answer. When the mother heard the words that stole away her final hope, she burst into crazed laughter. Her pain was beyond her strength. This laughter shook Kristian to the core.

It occurred to him that he needed to do something, but he didn't know what. The crazed woman laughed wildly and harrowingly until she disappeared like a ghost from Kristian's doorway.

She laughed on her way home and the local children began to follow her. Her laughter was horrifying. At moments she would interrupt it with singing. She sang the song about the land of Seven Castles.

XXII

The Ratcatcher found her like this. He too was searching for Agnes to no avail. Instead of a mother, he found the ruin of someone who used to be. She sat in a corner and was playing with bright embroidery abandoned by Agnes. When the Ratcatcher entered, she boastfully and childishly showed him Agnes's work. Afterwards, she began to laugh again. The Ratcatcher took her by the hand. She tolerated the gesture patiently but she was unmoved. Her insanity was merciful.

The Ratcatcher waited patiently, convincing himself that perhaps a moment of clarity would come. What had happened to Agnes? He feared everything and knew nothing. The insane woman certainly had an answer. Did she know anything about Agnes's disappearance? Did she know everything?

The woman continued to laugh and play. At moments she babbled gentle and foolish words of love that had been hidden for many years behind silence and apathy. She was talking to the one who was no longer there. She caressed the embroidery as if it was her daughter's neck. The Ratcatcher waited and waited.

He took her by the hand and tried to persuade her to look him straight in the eye. She resisted at first but later she gave in. Her eyes looked at him as if she had just managed to pull off a successful prank. And then she burst out into laughter once more.

The Ratcatcher did not allow himself to be confused by this. He looked sternly into the mother's evading eyes.

"Where is Agnes?" he asked commandingly.

She began to laugh once more.

He squeezed the mother's hand even harder and the look in his eyes made her scattered thoughts begin to fall back in line.

"Agnes left," the old woman laughed in a cruel manner. "Agnes left for the land of Seven Castles."

"Where is this land of Seven Castles?"

"Go to Koppel Mountain," the insane woman said. "Perhaps she is waiting there."

Then she burst into an untamed laughter that brought chills to the Ratcatcher's spine. He remembered the fairy tale about the land of Seven Castles. He remembered the evening he spent with Agnes when, with a smile and sleepy eyes, she told him about the fairy tale. He suddenly understood that this was the end. He had allowed Agnes to be taken and Tall Kristian took her. He allowed Agnes to leave and she left. It had always been the same.

A hopeless sorrow clenched his beating heart. He was suffocating beneath his own pain. Then, suddenly, his hand instinctively reached and felt something. He touched his fife.

How could he have forgotten about his fife? Why, it was the source of all his power and magic. Hadn't Agnes suggested on their first night that he blow into this instrument with all of his might? Back then, he was cautious but now times had changed. Now, only the fife had the power to ease his pain or drown out the terrible laughter of the insane woman. Nothing else could bring revenge to Hamelin. Oh, let the aldermen gab about their one hundred Rhine ducats! They were not the reason why the Ratcatcher's fife was about to sound.

XXIII

The Ratcatcher began to play his fife. It was no longer a thin muffled tone that lured rats. The sound was now full and powerful. A person's heart would begin to pound fiercely while it was playing. One's steps instinctively would begin to move faster and everything that slept deep within would begin to quietly awaken. But this song rapidly moved from one's dream into real life and from real life into death. Oh how tragic and vast was this tune! What a touching unforgettable voice it had!

The Ratcatcher continued to play.

The insane woman heard the sound of the fife. Her laughter grew cold upon her lips and then disappeared. Then suddenly the last echo of her laughter came back—she burst into tears. Her tears flowed down her cheeks. It was as if Agnes herself was leading her by her hand saying:

"Come with me."

The mother followed the Ratcatcher.

The Ratcatcher took to the streets. His fife sounded

powerful. Folks who heard it fell victim to the Ratcatcher's temptation. They would leave their work and follow. They would leave words unfinished and follow.

Washerwomen were doing the laundry in the courtyard of Erhadt's home. They were young and fresh and they spoke of their lovers. But the Ratcatcher was playing his fife. They forgot about their white linens and lustful lovers and followed.

Frosch's workshop was filled with carpenters. They were building beds and boasting about the beauty of their loved ones. But the Ratcatcher's fife interrupted their work and conversations. They too followed the Ratcatcher.

The local matchmaker and florist Elsbeth was luring in the virtuous Susa Tölsch, an orphan and servant to Councilman Lambert. The matchmaker jingled gold coins in front of Susa to dazzle her, but just at the moment when the orphan was about to submit to the matchmaker's promises of a comfortable life and blissful future, they both heard the Ratcatcher's song. And Elsbeth and Susa followed the Ratcatcher.

The journeymen in Strumm's workshop were cutting precious cloth. But they heard the sound of the fife and they left behind precious materials and conversations about distant seas and enormous seaports. They began a journey toward the sound of the Ratcatcher's song. It was a sound that was tempting and at the same time sorrowful.

They passed by the Thirsty Man Tavern. Röger, the innkeeper, stood at the doorway wearing his short hat, always ready to bow and smile. Black Liza stood behind him hiding at times but always ready to render a smile filled with love. The Ratcatcher's fife swept Röger and Black Liza away like ferocious water takes away a riverbank.

The Ratcatcher's fife awakened old dreams and old sorrows.

A local debaucher leaned his head forward as the fife played. He could suddenly see his dead mother caressing the forehead of a long-gone curly haired boy that resembled himself. As the fife played, he saw his future empty, impoverished — a shameful old age!

The most unabashed temptress in town, Dora, was thinking about a young man with blue eyes with whom she used to make love. She remembered the death of another who she once betrayed, and she remembered those who came through her life afterwards. She remembered the contemptuous looks of those who timidly would sneak out before sunrise. She remembered the wrinkles she saw in the mirror when morning came. The Ratcatcher's fife ignited sparks and ashes that had died out long ago. It was returning everything that was dormant and forgotten.

The number of people who followed the Ratcatcher began to increase. The Town Hall soon grew empty. Oddly enough, even the aldermen followed him. The Holy Trinity Cathedral emptied. The priest, the altar boy, even the sexton followed — the penitents, wedding processions, people in mourning and people full of hope.

The Ratcatcher's fife continued to lure everyone out and the flock followed silently behind it — those weary hearts and pitiful souls dusted by the road, spoiled by sin. Within those hearts a pure desire of some sort suddenly awakened.

The Ratcatcher's fife began to cheer up. It spoke of white veils on the heads of brides. It spoke of laughter, children, and the purity of one's first dream. It spoke of many sins and many treacheries, of bilge and filth, of poverty and fatigue. And joyous humming was heard among the colorful procession of Hamelin's citizens who were following the Ratcatcher. There was no one who didn't understand. Yes, everyone was going to the land of Seven Castles. Yes, the land of Seven Castles awaited! It was possible to have a different life.

Everyone — men, women and children — were abandoning their shallow life in Hamelin for the hope that was promised by the Ratcatcher's fife. Mothers were embracing their infants more firmly than usual. It would be a better life, a more beautiful life. Old men who already had one foot in their graves suddenly increased the speed of their step. It was worth it to grab a few extra days, hours, even seconds of a beautiful life!

XXIV

Only Sepp Jörgen stood there and did not follow. He saw the horde walking behind the Ratcatcher. He heard the promising and hopeful sounds. But he did not feel the same as the crowd. The fife did not speak to him. He let everyone from Hamelin pass as if he was loyal to his own destiny. His hungry eyes were looking for Kätchen and Lora, but to no avail.

Sepp Jörgen, whose destiny was always to understand things too late, was once again left alone. The flock of Hamelin's citizens passed him by like everything else passed by in his life. The crowd followed the song of the Ratcatcher's fife. Oh how beautiful this land of Seven Castles must be if the desire to seek it could awaken so many sleeping people!

The Ratcatcher's fife thundered and whispered. It cried and shouted with joy. It promised unknown pleasures and pure happiness. And everyone who listened to it would believe. Mosse the Usurer, who never believed in anything that wasn't backed by collateral, suddenly believed in the fife.

The Ratcatcher's parade journeyed through all the streets of the town. At times the fife sounded as if the Ratcatcher was still searching for one more soul. Someone in the procession was missing and it wasn't Sepp Jörgen. The fife pleaded and gently heaved a wail. But the one who was missing never appeared.

The fife faltered only once. Perhaps it was gasping for breath while drowning in a pool of tears. But it was only for a short moment, and then it sounded clear and victorious again — celebrating the miracle of the land of Seven Castles.

Soon after, the procession abandoned Hamelin's gate. It started to climb the incline of Koppel Mountain. The sighing of the branches carried through the forest and above the heads of the marching listeners, who were coming by the thousands.

The Ratcatcher's fife sounded relentless. In the beginning one could sense that it was mocking everything and everyone. It was a mockery similar to that of the devil on the Holy Trinity Cathedral. In the beginning one could hear deep groans, as if someone's clumsy hand touched a painful heart. The fife would die down but never died out. Waves of passion and faith carried away all that was murky and confusing. The road was clear. Everything seemed clear.

The Ratcatcher walked, and it seemed as if he grew

taller from the song that he played. He was tall, but at that moment he was a head taller than the rest of the crowd.

Oh the power of the Ratcatcher's fife! Hamelin was experiencing a rebirth. The fife awakened worlds that were long dead. It ignited hearts that were long dormant. The folks of the good Hanseatic town of Hamelin no longer thought about bargaining, profit or loss. They began to have desires unknown to them. They began to dream about things they had never dreamed before. Oh how powerful was the Ratcatcher's fife!

Was the Ratcatcher reborn by his fife as well? He no longer thought of his petty revenge, his minuscule anger. He no longer thought of Frosch and Strumm. He didn't even think about Tall Kristian. He could feel pain, but the longing for his love was much stronger in him.

The fife's song cleansed the Ratcatcher of his pain. It cleared the thought of Agnes from his mind. Oh the land of the Seven Castles!

His heart was still dreaming about Agnes, but the fife made her real. The sound of the fife was powerful and clear!

And the Ratcatcher repeated, "I feel no guilt or sin."

The road was clear and so was its end. Was it no longer necessary to jump into the abyss in order to reach

Eden? Agnes took this road, he thought to himself. He would catch up to her. He would find Agnes.

The people of Hamelin followed their dark and pensive leader, guided by the commanding and powerful song of his fife. It would excite its victims as it lured them to the gate of the land of Seven Castles.

Rain or shine, nothing could keep them from following the Ratcatcher. They would stumble, but they would rise up and carry on. All that they heard was the Ratcatcher's music. All that they saw was the Ratcatcher. And as they walked, the abyss suddenly opened up to them.

The Ratcatcher reached the abyss and stood over it. He looked more somber and melancholic than before. His fife sounded powerful and jubilant. No one stopped short of this gate. No one except Sepp Jörgen, who remained hovering pensively over the river's surface. As the fife played, everyone passed by the Ratcatcher with a smile of faith and their arms open wide. Oh land of Seven Castles! Everybody passed through and disappeared without a trace. Their sullen and silent leader continued to play and play. The crowd thinned and soon the Ratcatcher stood alone above the abyss.

He thought of that "yes" uttered one spring evening.

He thought of Agnes, who preceded him on this journey, but with whom he could reunite.

He leaned over the abyss.

And then there was silence — a strange silence. The fife suddenly fell out of the Ratcatcher's hands. His fife was his life. Its voice led the Ratcatcher just as it led the crowd that followed him, but as his fife fell downward its voice gradually faded into the abyss.

"Yes," the Ratcatcher answered. He too was searching for a gate to the Seven Castles, and when he reached it, he entered.

And that was how the Ratcatcher vanished along with the folks in Hamelin. And to this day, no one knows for certain whether any of them reached the land of Seven Castles.

XXV

The river keeps flowing; it flows untouched by the destinies of others.

A fishing boat rocked upon the river but the Fisherman inside did not think to cast his nets into the water. Instead, Sepp Jörgen sat idly in his boat and pondered over something that troubled him.

It was hard to explain why he was so sad. He still did not understand what had just happened in Hamelin, but he did suspect that something had changed. The world was suddenly silent, oddly silent. It was Sunday, and by then the cathedral was supposed to sound its bells for the benediction, but the bells never rang. It was Sunday, and by then Hamelin's merchants along with their wives, sons, and daughters were supposed to be strolling along the riverbank. But no one was sitting by the dykes. It was Sunday morning when all the well-dressed lads and giddy lasses would traditionally make fun of Sepp Jörgen. But no one was there that day to ridicule the Fisherman. And Jörgen, who sensed a change in the air, slowly began to understand that something extraordinary had happened. He remembered the horde of people from Hamelin following the Ratcatcher. He remembered the Ratcatcher's pale face.

Sepp Jörgen grabbed the oars and directed his boat to the riverbank. He anchored it and headed for town.

The streets were empty and the shops were abandoned. Jörgen walked through an archway that ordinarily would have been bustling with life, but on that day there was no sign of a living soul.

Jörgen's steps sounded somewhat ominous upon the cold cobblestones. He stopped at a church and it seemed odd to him that no beggar stood in front of its entrance. The Fisherman entered. The church was deserted and Jörgen's steps sounded even more ominous inside than on the street. He sprinkled a bit of holy water upon himself, but his eyes could still see nothing but emptiness. The benches were empty and the altar had no priest in front. Beneath the church's vault lay such silence that Jörgen thought he could hear the conversation between two angels huddled together above the altar. The sound of his own steps frightened him. He began to tiptoe, but even that motion continued to disturb the cursed silence.

Jörgen eventually realized that he was standing alone, face to face with the man on the cross. Everyone else had gone away. He was the last man in Hamelin—the last of the town's citizens.

The astonishment of that thought almost leveled the Fisherman. He barely reached the stairway, which led to the church's empty pulpit.

The sounds of the Ratcatcher's fife were slowly coming to life in the Fisherman's memory. Those faded tones were finally embracing him. The magic that overpowered the people of Hamelin began to overpower the Fisherman in spite of the fact that he outlived even the maker of this magic.

Jörgen began to track down the footsteps of the Ratcatcher and those who followed him. As he walked, the sound of the Ratcatcher's fife grew stronger.

XXVI

Then suddenly Sepp Jörgen could hear everything the people of Hamelin had heard — the sorrow, the pity, even the hope. He could hear a song embraced in tragedy and a song with an even more tragic ending. But just as he was about to leave the gates of Hamelin, he suddenly caught wind of a voice that no one among those who vanished ever noticed. It was the piercing sound of a baby's lament echoing through the open window of a quiet little house.

An abandoned infant was crying and Sepp Jörgen realized that he was not the last person in Hamelin, after all. And though it was unusual for him, this was something he realized at once.

He opened the door and entered the abandoned house. There, in a cradle, lay a plump little child who was only slightly covered with a blanket. The child was helplessly turning itself over and kicking the walls of its cradle. It was punching its fists randomly into the air. Its lament sounded like a clear command that until now could not be heard by anyone in this empty town, empty home, and empty room.

Sepp Jörgen stood there helplessly. What could he do for this child? It was hungry. How could he calm its hunger? When the child heard Jörgen's steps, it began to cry more fiercely. The Fisherman leaned over the cradle and took the infant into his arms. It was a girl.

He cradled her and, as he stood over this hungry child, he finally realized what had just happened in Hamelin. The streets were empty. Kätchen and Lora were gone. The crowd had left with the Ratcatcher. And then, once again, from somewhere deep inside, he heard a sorrowful and pitiful melody; and then one full of joy and victory.

He looked around the empty room once more only to notice the unfinished dishes left from a modest lunch. There was nothing that would soothe the hunger of an infant who was searching in vain for her mother's breast.

With a rough and untrained voice, Jörgen sang a lullaby for children in Hamelin—the song about the land of Seven Castles. He sang and cradled the infant.

But the child began to cry again. It wanted to feed. It did not know any other desire. The child's crying blended with the breath of the Ratcatcher's song—a song that the Fisherman could finally fully hear. Both songs blended into a fierce current that swept Jörgen off his feet. All the destitution and shame he had endured in his past life suddenly were unveiled before him.

Sepp Jörgen walked with the child into the streets. His pain and desires were luring him up toward Koppel Mountain to join the others, to join the Ratcatcher. He began to ascend the mountain with his little burden as if he was just about to lessen his load.

He never looked back after abandoning the gates of Hamelin. What did he care about a town that had given him nothing but wounds and ridicule? Jörgen's heart also craved the land of Seven Castles. His heart, too, dreamed of a different life, which suddenly seemed to be within arm's reach. The Ratcatcher and almost all of Hamelin had already found their way. Why couldn't Jörgen do the same?

The last man in Hamelin arrived at the gate to the land of Seven Castles. The abyss opened wide before him. In its depth lay a path that uttered tempting and pleasant words.

What is there to seek in Hamelin, or for that matter, in your Fatherland, dear Fisherman? Your desires have been futile! Your love has been futile! Your dreams have been futile! What fruits has your labor brought you? What are the limits of your abilities? What will your death accomplish? You pillage the river, Fisherman, but your spoils are pitiful! The land of Seven Castles awaits you! Another life is waiting for you there! No one will ever ridicule Sepp Jörgen. Neither Kätchen nor Lora will ever run from you. Oh Fisherman, the bare arms of women are eagerly waiting to embrace you!

But something unexpected suddenly happened — a child's cry overpowered the sound of the Ratcatcher's fife. The infant in Jörgen's arms was still crying. She wanted to feed. She knew nothing of the land of Seven Castles. And as she cried, her lament touched the last man in Hamelin and defeated his desires. Sepp Jörgen helplessly bid farewell to the abyss and to those who had vanished forever.

He then turned around and went to find a nursemaid who would be able to feed the starving infant.

Afterword

By Rajendra Chitnis, Ph.D.

Viktor Dyk's nameless Ratcatcher deserves a privileged place among the ambiguous, alienated anti-heroes of European Modernist fiction, as a relative of the anonymous narrator of Knut Hamsun's *Hunger* (1890) and forebear of figures like Franz Kafka's K. and Josef K., Robert Musil's Ulrich and Elias Canetti's Peter Kien. International readers' expectations of Czech literature in the inter-war period were, however, regrettably restricted mainly to the simple pleasures of Karel Čapek and Hašek's *Good Soldier Švejk*, and Dyk's short novel, first published in serialized form in 1911-12, was only translated into German (in Prague) in 1962 and into French in 2010. It reaches English-speaking readers for the first time now.

The novel is based on an old German legend, best known to English-speaking readers through the 1816 Brothers Grimm story *The Children of Hameln* and Robert Browning's 1842 dramatic lyric, *The Pied Piper of Hamelin*. In the legend, the ratcatcher uses his pipe to lure rats from the town into the river. When the townspeople refuse to pay him, he uses his pipe to lure Hamelin's children into a nearby mountain. Dyk's narrator, however, explicitly rules out the townspeople's failure to pay as the reason for his Ratcatcher's action: "Oh, let the aldermen gab about their one hundred Rhine ducats. They were not the reason why the Ratcatcher's fife was about to sound." Dyk thus frees the reader to consider afresh why at least this incarnation of the Hamelin ratcatcher is motivated to take such a terrible revenge.

As the title suggests, the novel form allows Dyk to develop and explore the character of the Ratcatcher. From the outset, Dyk presents him as a mysterious, potentially sinister outsider, speaking from the darkened street through the door of a local woman's dimly lit house. By declaring in the opening lines that he has no name, he establishes the quintessentially Modernist theme of the search for identity. The woman, Agnes, is immediately attracted to this exotic, at once imposing and somewhat lost stranger and his implicitly magical pipe, and so begins their love affair, an original addition to the traditional story, inspired perhaps by Goethe's short poem *Der Rattenfänger* (1803), in which the ratcatcher is said to be also "ein Mädchenfänger" (a maiden-catcher). For innocent, upstanding Agnes, the Ratcatcher is an erotic figure, who promises an escape from cold, stolid Hamelin into mystery and adventure, though increasingly he also seems to embody a kindness and sensitivity lacking in her other suitor, Tall Kristian. For the Ratcatcher, who compares himself to the legendary Ahasver, the Jew cursed to wander the earth for mocking Christ on the cross, Agnes represents the possibility of ending his restlessness and finding love and a home. The Ratcatcher's inability to decide between Agnes and continuing his journey recalls Hamlet, a parallel that intensifies as the love affair reaches its unhappy climax.

The initial description of the Ratcatcher seems to simultaneously evoke stereotypical images of both Hamlet and the 1890s Decadent poet. He is tall and thin, with feminine hands and an aristocratic demeanour belying his vagabond way of life. He wears a velvet jacket and tight-fitting leggings, which at least in the twilight appear to be black. His fife seems to be a metaphor for his artistic talent, a talent that he senses could be very powerful and destructive, but which he lacks the courage to test to the full. The ratcatcher had appeared as a metaphor for the Decadent artist, in the eleventh poem of the major Symbolist cycle *A Vengeful Cantilena* (*Mstivá kantilena*, 1898) by Karel Hlaváček (1874-1898). In the late 1890s, as an emerging writer, Dyk had been close to those associated with the leading Czech Decadent periodical, *Moderní revue*. Hlaváček's influence is evident in the language and imagery of Dyk's early verse, and Dyk published a touching essay-eulogy following Hlaváček's untimely death. Hlaváček's ratcatcher, arguably the only happy character in *A Vengeful Cantilena*, buys rats from villagers, then rides out into the fields to sell them to starving rebels. Artist-figures, including the narrator, are linked throughout the cycle by the motif of red hair, an ironic allusion to the notion that artists have access to higher, mystical knowledge; the ratcatcher ties up his ghastly mare with a fox-brush. Like the poet-narrator, who presents himself as an ironic observer as civilization crumbles and the rebellion inevitably fails, the ratcatcher stands aloof, nonchalantly feeding off the disintegration and despair.

Dyk's implied author does not identify with his ratcatcher in the same way. Unlike many writers in this period, Dyk does not ironize or mock his central character, and only distances himself from him towards the end. He shares the Ratcatcher's disdainful, implicitly Decadent rejection of small-minded materialism, embodied by the artisans of Hamelin, and understands his quest for a more noble way of living. The implied author's sympathies, however, come to lie equally with the contrasting figure of Sepp Jörgen, who catches fish, not rats. Like the Ratcatcher, Sepp is an outsider, who lives alone in poverty on the edge of town, scorned and mocked by the good people of Hamelin. The Ratcatcher – like the narrator – also treats Sepp condescendingly, but recognizes him as a victim of the thoughtless cruelty of Hamelin, and even attempts to express the affinity between them when he says: "You will never be happy [...] Perhaps you are destined for something better." As the narrator frequently reiterates, Sepp's apparent failing is his slowness to grasp the meaning of situations; he is a mental equivalent of the lame boy in the Grimm and Browning versions of the story, who is too slow to catch the crowds bewitched by the Ratcatcher's fife. At the end of the story, in the wake of the Ratcatcher's act of nihilism, the implied author's sympathies transfer decisively to Sepp, who finds an abandoned baby girl and goes in search of someone to feed her.

For Czech critics, this shift of sympathy from the

Ratcatcher to the fisherman reflects a change in Dyk's attitude to writing, which he repeatedly dramatizes in his work from the early 1910s. In his "Poetic prologue from 1912", he writes: "I am changed, yes, my faith is different [...] / He who once negated many things now no longer negates [...] / The dark vermin that gathered like screech-owls on a tower has fled / I used to knock down and now I would like to build." In this prologue, in the epic poem *Giuseppe Moro* (1911) and in the plays *Don Quixote Grows Wise* (*Zmoudření Dona Quijota*, 1911) and *The Great Magician* (*Veliký mág*, 1914), Dyk characterizes this change in terms of youth and maturity. The youthful artist is driven by implacable idealism, marked by impatience and hubris. The consequences may be tragic, as in the cases of the young sea-farer Giuseppe Moro or the Ratcatcher, or comical, as in the case of Dyk's Don Quixote, who says ruefully on his death-bed: "I imagined everything differently. We must, however, be reconciled with reality and see things as they really are [...] My whole past is just a foolish and ridiculous dream. Now it is time to wake up."

Dyk suggests in *The Ratcatcher* that the inability to reconcile proud idealism with base reality leads through skepticism to despair. Whereas in Hlaváček's *A Vengeful Cantilena*, vengeance is futile but vaguely noble, in *The Ratcatcher* it is merely a self-destructive gesture of defeat. For Dyk, the contemporary mature artist finds a path down the apparent lofty impasse of Decadence and "art for art's sake" to constructive engagement with the needs of those around him. At the same time, Dyk suggests that the artist must use his gifts wisely. Like the Ratcatcher with his pipe, he has the capacity to enchant his audience, to bring to life their deepest hopes and dreams, to make them followers in the pursuit of an ideal that is in fact an illusion. In Dyk's version, it is not just the children, but above all the adults, who fall under the Ratcatcher's spell.

The model embodied by Sepp should not be confused with the practical, pragmatic approach – the "mundane work" - advocated to the Czech nation by the first Czechoslovak president, Tomáš Garrigue Masaryk and his adherents. Throughout his life, Dyk proved one of Masaryk's fiercest and most articulate opponents; he identified Masaryk's ideas with Hamelin-like petty bourgeois materialism, caution and lack of ambition, which diminished the nation and its aspirations for itself. Like the great Czech novelists of the inter-war period, Jaroslav Durych (1886-1962) and Vladislav Vančura (1891-1942), Dyk inherited from the Czech fin-de-siècle a perception of the contemporary

Czech nation as timid, fractious and impotent. While Durych sought recovery in renewed Christian piety and Vančura in communism, Dyk strove to nurture a secular national solidarity and activism founded on self-sacrificing devotion and a belief in the nation's past glory and future strength. In this context, we might therefore best understand the orphaned, wailing infant in need of nourishment as a metaphor for the nation, while Sepp (whose name is a Germanized Pepík, or Czech "average Joe") represents the clumsy, limited but intuitively well-intentioned contemporary Czech writer, who is taking his first steps towards renewal, but is yet to find a voice. Indeed, given his proximity to Nature, Sepp foreshadows in embryo the rough-hewn, taciturn hero of Hamsun's Nobel-Prize-winning 1917 novel, *Growth of the Soil*, who transforms virgin Norwegian wilderness into a thriving, resilient family farm.

In a further reflection of Dyk's turn from Decadence to conservative nationalism, *The Ratcatcher* also suggests that influences from outside – embodied by the Ratcatcher – find Czech culture inhospitable and infertile and ultimately only cause harm. Like Hamelin, the Czech nation needs to look for the source of recovery within itself. With respect to the underwhelming Sepp, one cannot help but be reminded of the advice given to the Czech nation by the prophetess, Libuše, in one of the oldest works of Czech literature, the so-called *Dalimil Chronicle* (c.1314), to choose a leader, however ugly, drawn from their own, rather than look abroad. Dyk's position contrasts with the cosmopolitan aesthetics of the Paris-influenced inter-war left-wing Avant-garde, quintessentially expressed by Vítězslav Nezval (1900-58) in his 1922 poem *The Marvelous Magician* (*Podivuhodný kouzelník*). Nezval here also addresses the tension between idealism and illusion through the frame of magic and the superhuman, and a comparison of his magician, inspired by the legend of Merlin, with Dyk's Ratcatcher would reveal much about the shifting sands of Czech and indeed European Modernism.

Despite these rich local contexts, *The Ratcatcher* is not a parochial work, but addresses the cultural situation facing intellectuals throughout Europe at the beginning of the twentieth century. A key moment is the encounter between the Ratcatcher and Faustus in the aptly named Thirsty Man. Faustus sees in the Ratcatcher a fellow seeker of knowledge, who places his quest above domestic comfort and pleasure. In the scene, however, Faustus effectively takes the role of Mephistopheles, tempting the Ratcatcher to embrace the power he has within him: "The things you could do

with your pipe! You could be master of life and death."
The scene is ambiguous: is Faustus a self-deluding
buffoon, or are his contemporary successors, typified
by the Ratcatcher, merely incapable of imagination and
higher vision? Dyk shows here how, at the turn of the
twentieth century, the confident, early modern dream
of mastery of the world through knowledge, embodied
by Faustus, dissolves for the Modernist intellectual
into hesitation and doubt. Faustus's journey of
discovery becomes aimless, futile wandering, and
the noble figure of the artist as a seeker of knowledge
and bearer of wisdom will soon be replaced by men
without qualities: the hack writer, the bureaucrat, the
land surveyor, the librarian. According to Faustus,
what hinders the Ratcatcher is his heart, which draws
him back to Agnes and his fellow human beings. In the
light of the Ratcatcher's final act, the encounter may
therefore be read as a prescient tabling of the question
whether the catastrophes of the coming decades will
arise from an absence or a surfeit of compassion. Here,
as throughout the novel, nervous uncertainty prevails,
countered only by Dyk's fragile, concluding hope
that an uneducated native son can begin the work of
reunifying heart and mind and rebuilding civilization.

ABOUT THE AUTHOR

Viktor Dyk was born in 1877 in Pškov near Mělník. He was a prominent Czech writer, poet, playwright, literary translator, political writer and politician. He completed a degree in law at Charles University in Prague. In 1907 he became an editor for the magazine *Lumír*, a literary journal that sought to elevate Czech literature to a global level. As a member of the Constitutional Progressive Party, he entered politics in 1911 when he ran as candidate for election to the Imperial Council. For his subversive writings advocating the secession of Bohemia and Moravia from the Austro-Hungarian Empire, Dyk was jailed in Vienna from 1916 until 1917. In 1918 he became one of the founding members of the Czechoslovak National Democracy Party, a conservative nationalist political party. In 1920 he was elected as a member of parliament and often opposed the policies of Tomáš Garrigue Masaryk, the first president of Czechoslovakia. As a politician, Viktor Dyk continued to write. He was an editor for the *Narodní Listy* (National Leaflets), a conservative newspaper. He died of a heart attack in 1931 while vacationing by the Adriatic Sea in Croatia.

CPSIA information can be obtained
at www.ICGtesting.com
Printed in the USA
FFOW04n1123130215
11072FF